I Blame the Alcohol

Jade Everhart

To my father,
Who taught me I can accomplish anything I want as long as
I set my mind to it and work hard.

Prologue

♥

6 months earlier...

Cody

Smack! The medicine ball bounces off the wall and hurtles into the hands of the smallest girl I have ever seen. Actually, I take that back. She may be short, but she certainly isn't small. At least not in the traditional sense.

Smack! The mini powerhouse continues to lay waste to the exercise ball, causing other gym patrons to look her way. Taber's fitness centre is never busy before 6am, so it's easy to pick out the early-morning regulars.

This girl isn't a regular.

I study her from across the gym, dominance and discipline oozing from her every pore. The tight black tank top and camo leggings show off a figure that could be used in biology class to mark all the muscles on the human body. I'm no stranger to fit individuals, hell only the most dedicated roll their asses out of bed before dawn, but this girl is a whole other level.

Finishing her round of wall balls, the girl drops the medicine ball and stalks over to the climbing cage. I stare, intrigued, as the fitness guru starts assembling boxes below the pull up bar. With a quick glance at her smart watch, the girl bounds up the makeshift stairs, latching onto the bar overhead, and proceeds to rip off pull ups like there's no tomorrow.

"Holy shit." The guy doing bicep curls next to me almost drops the dumbbells he's holding as he watches the platinum pixie repeatedly heave her chin above the bar. I nod in silent agreement, watching the girl lightly drop to her feet and march over to start the wall balls again.

Wow.

Taber's fitness centre has two floors: the upper allocated to the indoor track and cardio machines lining the walls while the bottom floor is split in two, one side for free range exercises with stretching mats and a climbing cage, while the other side contains dumbbells, barbells, squat racks, and any other heavy lifting equipment you can think of. From what I've seen this year, most early birds stick to either the track upstairs or the weights on the bottom floor. Until today, I hadn't seen anyone use the free-range space, let alone the climbing cage. Especially during the ungodly hours before dawn.

There is an unspoken rule among regulars that when someone's in the zone, you don't intrude. We're all here because of stubborn willpower, and honestly, no one feels like making conversation before breakfast. I've never considered this etiquette to be a hindrance before, but now I wish I was unaware of its existence so I could wander over and introduce myself.

I drag out my dumbbell set for as long as possible, hoping the new girl will finish up her workout so we can not-so-accidentally bump into each other on the way out. But despite my best efforts, there's only so many variations of tricep dips you can do before it starts to look stupid, so, accepting defeat, I bend to scoop up my things and head towards the exit. Taking one last glance at the mystery girl, I find dark blue eyes staring back at me.

I've never been known for being smooth, or charming for that matter, but the water bottle fumble I do next is enough to make even the most confident guy cringe. Doing my best to recover, I tuck the traitorous bottle against my chest and send a quick wave towards the girl watching me with an amused smile.

And this is why gym regulars keep to themselves.

Mentally cursing my newfound clumsiness, I give Stephen, the front desk attendant, a nod on my way out and hurry back to my dorm. There's a pile of homework I need to get done before attending the lacrosse banquet tonight, but as I walk across Taber's manicured lawns, the only thing I can think about is how the girl's topknot looked when it was coming undone.

Screw gym etiquette, next time I see her, I'm going over to introduce myself.

***

"Don't even think about crying on me, Ellsworth. I did not mentor your ass all year just for you to crumble the second I leave." Mo's voice rings out over the chaotic chatter and with a laugh, I give him a shove.

"Dream on, old man. There are no tears here."

Chuckling, Mo throws an arm around my shoulders and steers me around the room. I haven't stopped smiling since being titled Rookie-of-the-Year and that was before Mo announced I was taking his place as team captain next year.

Me. Team captain. Taking over from Taber's very own lacrosse legend, my friend and mentor, The Great Mighty Mo.

The announcement went over as well as can be expected, the seniors who have been working their asses off for the last four years were pissed, but there's nothing they can do. If anyone but Mo had made my captain status official, there would have been some serious backlash, but given it was Taber's graduating all-star, no one was brave enough to voice their opposition. So far, anyways.

I already know next year will be a challenge. There will be a lot of doubters, some potential retaliation once Mo's gone, but I will stand my ground. Mo picked me for a reason, and I will prove to each and every one of them that I deserve this position. Even if it kills me.

"Congrats, Cody." Mason claps me on the back as Mo and I pass him on our victory tour. His praise seems genuine, though chances are it's more for the fact a defenseman finally won an award over the forward players. We both play defence, and part of the role is accepting the guys who score the goals are the ones who get the glory. The running joke on the team is the forwards score the points, the ladies, and the trophies while the defensemen support the line.

It's not like all us defensemen are bitter, it's simply the way it goes.

Well, until today that is.

"There is someone I want you to meet."

Mo guides me away from our teammates, their rowdiness increasing with the alcohol level. Most of the parents have started to head out, so my teammates are downing the spiked punch like there's no tomorrow.

If there's one thing small universities are good at, it's throwing after parties. And considering our team just broke the school's consecutive championship streak with a fifth banner for Taber University's repertoire this year, tonight's party is bound to be a big one.

I spy a pretty blonde in a green dress that immediately makes me think of the girl from the gym this morning. I do a double take, thinking it might be her, but the brown eyes that smile my way don't trigger the recognition I was hoping for.

Disappointment tugs at my chest when I suddenly realize Mo has been talking to me this whole time, "...starting at Taber this fall. You consider me a brother, don't you Ellsworth?"

"Of course." I answer with as much confidence as possible, instantly feeling bad for tuning him out. Forcing my eyes to stop their fruitless search, I turn my full attention onto my graduating captain.

"Good, because I consider you a brother as well. And family never abandons family." Mo's words spread warmth through my chest and I can't hold back the smile that creeps across my face.

"So, because you're taking my place next year, I expect you to fill my shoes both on and off the field. You get what I'm saying?"

I nod, determined to make my mentor proud, "I'll look after the team, Mo. On and off the field."

Mo nods, leading us towards the dessert table. The chocolate fountain is a fan favourite, and the line to dip assorted fruit snakes across the back of the room.

"I'm happy to hear it. Of course, being my replacement means you'll also have to keep an eye out for Stella next fall."

"Stella?"

We slow as we approach the table, students waving us ahead as if Mo's performance these last five years has made him an exception to standing in line. Leisurely grabbing a plate full of strawberries, Mo takes his time dipping each one, pushing his priority status to the maximum. I shift from foot-to-foot, uncomfortably aware of the people patiently waiting their turn.

"My younger sister. You're going to need better listening skills if you're going to lead our team to victory next year."

My shoulders hunch with embarrassment as I hurry to apologize, "I'm sorry Mo, I've been distracted all day."

Finally taking leave of the chocolate fountain, Mo sends a smirk my way, "Is the distraction female by any chance?"

"Maybe. There was this girl at the gym today who I've never seen before. I'm just curious about what her deal is." I shrug as if said girl hasn't been haunting me since 5am this morning.

"You should ask her out." Mo impatiently checks his phone as he chews on a strawberry. I sigh, not wanting to explain the gym code situation. The more I think about it, the more ridiculous I feel. Why didn't I just go over and say hello?

"Well, first I've got to talk to her, but once I do that..." My words die off as platinum hair materializes in front of me. I blink once, twice, thinking she will disappear, but she doesn't.

Out of the topknot, the girl's platinum hair hangs down to her waist, delicate braids intricately weaved throughout. The black dress she's wearing hits mid-thigh, her toned legs flexing under the banquet hall's lighting. I gulp as my eyes trail up to her face, the sparkly eye makeup making her eyes look like the deepest part of the Pacific Ocean.

My mouth goes dry as I stare at the girl in front of me.

It's her. It's the girl from this morning.

"Ellsworth, I want you to meet my younger sister, Stella. She won't be part of the lacrosse team next year, but I expect you to watch over her like you would any other player." My stomach drops as his words sink in. The girl from the gym is Mo's sister.

His *younger* sister.

"I'm not a pet Mo, I don't need to be looked after." Stella rolls her eyes, completely unaware of the turmoil raging inside my body.

Mo sighs, equally oblivious, "I know you don't, but I'll feel better knowing someone is looking out for you. And Ellsworth is the best, you know I wouldn't trust your wellbeing to just anyone." Pricks of guilt needle my gut as Stella turns her fierce gaze onto mine.

"Don't get in my way, okay rookie?" Her biting words tug at my lips and I find myself holding out my hand for a shake.

"So long as you stay out of trouble, we won't have a problem. *Freshman.*" Her eyes narrow as she takes my hand and I fight to hold back a grin.

"We'll see about that." Her small hand fits perfectly in mine and for a moment I forget her older brother is standing just a few feet away.

"Alright, now that's out of the way, Stel, I think it's time we tear up the dance floor."

Mo's voice is like a bucket of cold water as I drop his sister's hand and take a step back. Her dark blue eyes flick to mine and the pull between us grows stronger. I take another step back and something flashes in those beautiful blue eyes. Before I can decipher it, Stella gives me a polite nod, links her arm through her brother's and together they head to the dance floor.

"You alright, Cap?" I hadn't noticed I was staring after the sibling pair until Mason walks by with a friendly nudge.

Dragging my eyes away from the girl I lost, found, and lost all over again, I turn and give my teammate a weary smile, "You don't have to call me that until next fall."

Mason cocks his head to the side, his flaming red hair flopping with the motion, "The second you stepped onto the lacrosse field this season, you were bound to be captain. We all knew it, Mighty was just the one to announce it."

He nods in Mo's direction, "It's about time someone took his place. Even if he wasn't graduating, it was time for him to go."

I frown as my protective instincts kick in, "Mo has done so much for this team, he will be leaving a legacy behind."

"Hey, all I'm saying is it was time for some fresh blood. And I cannot be happier you were the one chosen." Flashing me a grin, Mason motions to the blonde I mistook for Stella just moments earlier.

"That one has been eyeing you up all evening. Go have some fun, Cap. Tonight the defensemen are the ones scoring."

I sneak a glance at the girl in the green dress and find her staring back at me. A sly smile comes my way, and I find myself smiling back.

I start making my way over when Mo's laughter rings out over the crowd. I turn to see my mentor and his younger sister doing some sort of dance routine and the smile taking over Stella's face stops me dead in my tracks.

Wow.

Shaking my head, I resume my path towards the blonde and paste a polite smile onto my face. Her brown eyes are a far cry from the ones I wish they were, but you can't always get what you want.

Chapter 1

❤

Present day...

Stella

7.2. The treadmill beeps as I increase the speed, forcing me to lengthen my stride to keep from being thrown off the end. I sneak a glance at my neighbour's screen and feel a spark of satisfaction.

6.5. And he doesn't have any incline on.

My sweaty neighbour gets off the treadmill five minutes later, but I keep running for another twenty. It's one thing to beat your opponent, it's another to make a point. Because that's what happens when you stop growing at 4'11, people assume you're weak, or worst, *delicate*.

God, I hate that word. Just because I'm short doesn't mean I'm made of glass.

I bite back a sigh of relief when I finally press the cool down setting, my treadmill automatically reducing to a brisk walking pace. Sweat trickles down my neck and drips into my sports bra as I walk my heart rate down to normal levels.

I feel stares on my back as I chug my water bottle, and I resist the urge to tug at my tank top. The dark material is plastered against my skin, but that doesn't stop me from glancing down to make sure both sides of my torso are covered. All clear.

Content everything is covering what it should be, I hop off the treadmill and walk over to the water station. I glance around the room, hoping for a sight I haven't seen in a while.

Well, more like *someone* I haven't seen in a while.

The usual pre-dawn regulars are dispersed around the lower floor, but the blonde fauxhawk I'm looking for is nowhere in sight. With a sigh, I turn from the water station and head over to the cubby holding my gym bag.

If someone asked me why I worked out for an extra hour today, I'd be hard pressed to admit the truth. It's not like me to wait around for a guy, hoping he'll make an appearance. Even if the guy in question does have shoulders that could rival the rocky mountains.

"Weird not seeing Cody around, hey?" The friendly voice drags my attention to the front desk, where Stephen has been working since before I started at Taber University. His unruly dark curls put a smile on my face even as disappointment weighs down on my chest.

"I heard he got the okay to start exercising last week, so I'm sure he will be back any day now."

The fact he still hasn't made an appearance is starting to concern me. Not that it's a personal concern, it's more of a hope-he's-okay-because-he-is-one-of-my-brother's-closest-friends concern. There's a difference, trust me.

"Man, I hope so. I miss watching you two bicker every morning. Makes my day feel so much more productive." Stephen shoots me a wink and I let out a laugh. Cody and I have a tendency to argue like an old married couple over everything and anything. I didn't realize how much I enjoyed sparring with him until he got injured.

"Things will be back to normal before you know it. See you later, Stephen!"

I nudge my bag higher on my shoulder and head towards the door. The guy I outran on the treadmill earlier quickly drops his dumbbells and rushes over to intercept my path. I sigh, preparing myself for the new routine that's taken place since Cody's been MIA in recovery.

"Hey." The smile sent my way is cute in a friendly way. Light blue eyes offset the brown hair, and the freckles dotting his nose are visible even from my standpoint.

"Hello." I smile politely and make a move for the door. Freckles takes a step to the left and blocks my trajectory.

Here we go again.

"Stella, right? I'm Hayden." I force my lips to stay in their upright position and shake his outstretched hand. His grip is rough, like he's trying to make up for the treadmill showdown he lost minutes earlier.

Too bad his cardio isn't as strong as his handshake.

"Nice to meet you, Hayden." I release his grip and try for the door again, hoping he will take the hint. A step to the right extinguishes all hope.

"I was wondering if maybe I could take you out for coffee some-time? I noticed your boyfriend isn't around anymore, so I figured you might finally be available..." He trails off and gives me a grin that I think is supposed to be charming. I stare at him for a couple beats, willing myself to feel the slightest bit intrigued.

Nope, I got nothing.

"That's very kind of you, but I'm afraid I'm really busy right now." I switch my gym bag to my other shoulder and nod towards the door.

"Busy with what?"

Doing anything but going for coffee with you. I bite back the words just in time and impatiently look at my watch. "Studying for exams. Speaking of which, I'm late for a study session with my roommate, so if you'll excuse me."

Without giving Hayden a chance to respond, I use my shoulder to push past him. If someone wants to block your path, break through them. That's my brother's motto, anyways. It always worked for him on the lacrosse field and as it turns out, it works well on romantic interests as well.

"Maybe after your exams?" The question hits my back, but I keep walking, pretending not to hear. Rude, I know, but thanks to the extended workout I'm hungrier than usual and Hayden is the fifth guy in the last two weeks who has approached me at the gym. It's like now that Cody is gone, it's open season for every other gym go-er.

The whole thing is ridiculous because Cody and I have never been a thing. Sure, we workout at the same time and bicker continuously, but we have never given any indication that we are dating.

God forbid Taber Tigers' lacrosse captain show any romantic interest in his mentor's younger sister.

I take my time walking back to my dorm because there is no way my roommate is awake yet, never mind ready to start our study session. Lou isn't necessarily a night owl, but she's certainly not a morning person like me. And with our first semester classes wrapping up as we head into exams, Lou will be wanting to get as much sleep as possible. She is the world's biggest procrastinator, so it's safe to say exam season isn't her favourite time of year.

Thankfully, the first-year dormitories are closest to the university, so I only have to brave the December cold for a lung-freezing three-minute walk. I take a deep breath as I reach the side door, bracing myself for the bitter wind before pushing it open.

Frozen crystals glitter on every surface in sight, Taber's manicured lawns hidden by a deep layer of snow. I quicken my pace as the air nips through my leggings, not taking a second to admire the row of pine trees lining either side of the courtyard or the crunch of fresh snow under my shoes.

I feel like an Olympic speed walker by the time I swipe my access card to my residence building, and I breathe a sigh of relief when warm air hits my face. Tugging out the elastic band holding my hair in place, my mind drifts back to the absent lacrosse captain.

I know for a fact Cody got cleared to resume training last week because Lou passed on the information from her admittedly gorgeous boyfriend, Wes, who is a rookie on the team this year.

So, the question becomes has Cody gone back to training and just forgone our pre-injury routine or has something else happened that I don't know about?

My heart and stomach clench simultaneously and I tell myself it's from the thought of Cody re-injuring himself.

Cody

"It's not looking good, Cody."

The face looking at me through the screen of my computer is drawn, the tone grave. My heart sinks, already knowing what's about to come.

"By the time Hank and I finish our last excursion, the first plane we can hop on will be in the New Year. And by then, we will only have three days together before your classes start for next semester." My mom's voice grows heavy as she wills me to understand.

Most of my traits come from my mother, but my people pleasing nature is probably the most prevalent of them all. Neither of us like disappointing the other, so I have no doubt this change of plan is hurting her just as much as it's hurting me.

"It doesn't make sense for you to hurry back just so we can have a few days together. Enjoy your stay in Hawaii, and I will send you pictures of my place all decked out for Christmas." I push a big smile to the surface so she can ease off the guilt.

"Are you sure? I feel so terrible... if I'd known Hank had booked the surprise getaway for over the holidays, I would have postponed. But the tickets are non-refundable so..." My mom's blonde hair, so similar to mine, shakes back and forth on the screen.

"Mom. It's fine. The doctor said I can start lifting again Wednesday, so I'll be back training so much that I won't even notice you're gone."

God, recovery has been a bitch. Just last week I was able to start running again, but the way I had to stop and suck down oxygen every five minutes made me feel like the worst varsity athlete ever, never mind a varsity captain.

"Well, if you're sure. I miss you."

"Miss you too." A genuine smile fills my face as we end the call. The next few weeks might get a little lonely, but at least my mother is finally getting to see Hawaii. It's been a lifelong dream of hers, but as a single mother she had to sacrifice frivolous things like international trips, so I am glad she's met someone like Hank who can give her those experiences she missed out on.

I close my laptop and sprawl on my bed. I could drive home to Lethbridge for the break, but then it would be just me rattling alone in our family home. That seems more depressing than simply staying in Taber, where I am close enough to the university that I can use the training field and gym whenever I want. And who knows, maybe a few of my players will be staying through the holidays as well.

With that hopeful thought, I sit up and scrounge the room for my phone. Finding it in my coat pocket, I unlock it and open my messages, pulling up a strand that hasn't been opened in a while.

STEL: Don't do something stupid like come back to the gym before the doctor clears you.

ME: Does this mean I'll have to bring a doctor's note?

STEL: Only if you plan on being stupid.

I grin rereading her responses. Normally, we see each other a minimum of five times a week, sometimes more if I don't have games on the weekend. But since I got plowed down during the season opener, I've seen Stella maybe six times over the last six weeks.

The worst part about recovery hasn't been losing my cardio to the point of humiliation, it's been not seeing my 4'11 gym buddy. I miss her, miss our futile arguments, miss seeing her topknot come loose after her workouts.

In a way, she is one of my closest friends here at Taber. If things were different, she would be marked down as my future wife, but they aren't, and I am mature enough to realize that what you want and what you are willing to sacrifice aren't always as cut and paste as they may seem.

My phone buzzes with an incoming call from my favourite rookie. It's unprofessional to have a favourite as the captain, but every captain has one. Wes is mine, and I was lucky enough to be Mo's.

I press accept and immediately Wes' voice fills the silence of my room, "Cap! It was so good to have you back last practice. Oh, and don't worry, we've all agreed not to talk about the fact Hunter kicked your ass during sprints."

Every captain has a favourite rookie, but they also have a least favourite. And that's Hunter for me. Not because he's a bad lacrosse player, but because he had the audacity to stick his tongue down Stella's throat right in front of me. It was dark, we were at a club, and I have no ownership over her, but that night permanently placed Hunter in my bad books.

"I appreciate the reminder, Wes."

"Hey, anytime." Despite myself, I feel my lips tug into a grin. Mo sometimes comes off as condescending, but Wes always manages to turn cockiness into charm.

"What can I help you with?" It wouldn't surprise me if that's all Wes called to tell me, but I have a feeling we're not done yet.

"So, now that you're feeling better, I was thinking we should throw a party to celebrate. Everyone was concerned alcohol and music would be too much for you, but now that you're getting slaughtered during sprints, we figured you might be up for a night out."

"Who would be hosting?" I ask the question wearily, remembering how long it took for me to clean up my house last time.

"Mason has offered, apparently his landlord relaxed some of the overnight guest rules, so a few of us can crash there if need be."

"Sounds good. When is the party?" I walk from my bedroom to the tiny office and check my calendar. Besides hitting the gym Wednesday morning, there's nothing written down for this week.

"Tomorrow night. I'll text you the address."

"Isn't a Tuesday a little eager for exam break?" I do a double take at my calendar, realizing a morning gym session isn't the only thing written down for that day.

"Not as eager as a barely recovered captain doing sprints last week. It'll be good fun, Cap. I'm bringing Trip, so I'm sure Stella will tag along." He drops her name innocently, but I know exactly what he's doing.

"Sounds good. I'll talk to you later." I end the call, using my other hand to trace the words carefully written down for Wednesday morning.

5am Taber Gym. See Stella.

Chapter 2

Stella

2 minutes remaining...

The three little words blinking on the bottom of my computer screen triggers my heart to pump harder than it did during this morning's workout. The exam's clock counts down the seconds remaining on my exam as I take one final breath and move my cursor to the submit button. Body odour of the strongest caliber fills my nostrils as the guy to my left swivels anxiously in his chair.

Swallowing the urge to gag, I sneak a glance over and see the poor guy made the mistake of wearing grey today on top of forgetting deodorant. The rancid smell coming from his underarms actually pales in comparison to the unfortunate stains running down either side of his torso.

Relatable.

With a heavy exhale, I press submit just as the timer starts flashing red. My screen returns to the home setting, sucking away the last two hours of brain power with a friendly reminder to swipe my access card on the way out.

Resisting the urge to flip off the cartoon tiger providing the animated message, I grab the items littering my desk and head out. I give Grey T-Shirt a supportive pat as I pass him by, and he acknowledges it with a defeated sigh.

Exam season gets to the best of us.

"How did it go?" Lou, who was waiting for me just outside the testing centre, shakes her wavy golden-brown hair out of her eyes as we start the walk back to our dorm.

I sigh, "It's probably better if we don't talk about it. That may have ruined my chances of making the Dean's List this semester." And if that's the case, father is not going to be pleased.

Why couldn't my older brother have been Taber's all-star lacrosse forward but a terrible student? Or even an average student? Did he really need a degree that said distinguished on it?

If it was easy, everyone would do it.

"I'm sure you did better than you think." Lou's voice flows over the one in my head, yanking me out of my spiralling thoughts.

"You're right, hon. Best to stay positive." I give her a big smile, hoping it will hide my grimace. The returning nose wrinkle tells me I didn't succeed.

"Good thing I have something that will cheer you up then." Lou's beautiful grey eyes turn up at the corners as a genuine smile takes over her face.

Excitement flows through my veins at her words, and unable to help myself, I clap my hands together and squeal in anticipation. Nothing beats surprises.

"Well, there's a lacrosse party happening at Mason's tonight, and I was wondering if you would want to be my plus one?" The excitement vibrating through me slows to a dull throb.

"A lacrosse party?" Throwing my hands on my hips, I whirl around to face my roommate, "Wouldn't that mean you are already someone else's plus one?"

A faint blush creeps along Lou's cheeks like it always does whenever someone mentions her boyfriend. It has managed to stay adorable since they started dating a couple of months ago, and I honestly can't imagine a day when Lou loses her signature relationship blush. My only complaint is now I have to share this amazing girl with another human being.

"I mean, Wes technically invited me, but he was adamant that you come along." Lou ducks her head, a telltale sign she's worried about upsetting me.

"And why would your sex-god of a boyfriend be so insistent I come along? Lord knows you two love your alone time." I already know the answer to my question, but sometimes it's fun to play along.

Plus, I can never miss out on an opportunity to poke fun at Lou's newly active sex life.

"Well, that is true..." The blush on her cheeks grows rosier as a cheeky grin splits her face. Bet you a thousand dollars she's thinking sinful thoughts right now.

Mama has never been prouder.

"But I think Wes wanted you to come for Cody. I mean, we will be together the whole time, but by the sounds of it, I think Caveman Cody misses you."

I snort a laugh at the nickname as well as the statement. If the captain missed me so much, then why didn't he reach out more? Or make up an excuse to see me?

He was worried what Mo would think.

The answer comes immediately but it doesn't reduce my annoyance one bit. Sometimes asking rhetorical questions is not the way to go. If you don't want the answer, don't ask the question.

Bet you can guess who taught me that motto.

"I highly doubt Caveman Cody missed my company, but if my sister wants my presence at this party, then I will gladly attend." A shy smile tugs Lou's lips at my use of the endearment.

"I would really love for you to come tonight, Stella. I'll even let you pick out my outfit."

"And do your hair?"

Lou gulps audibly and I bite back a laugh. I dressed her up as an eighty's rocker chick one time and she has never gotten over it. The matching leather pantsuits I'd picked out for us were uncomfortable, I'll admit, but that didn't stop us from winning the costume contest.

She puffs out a breath and nods tentatively, "And my hair."

I let out a small shriek of excitement, "I already have so many ideas of what look I want to try on you."

Lou tries to give me a smile but this time it's her turn to grimace.

∞

"Real talk: Do we want to give Wes an immediate erection or just enough of a tease that he will carry you off to bed and worship you for hours later?"

Lou props herself up with one of my pillows, the red velvet comforter shifting smoothly beneath her.

"Should I be concerned about the use of "we" in this scenario?"

I wave off her comment over my shoulder, not bothering to turn my attention from my open closet.

"I am simply an invested third-party observer, think of me as your fairy godmother who helps you get laid. I do the prep work, Wes does the real work, and you reap the benefits."

Biting on her lip to keep from laughing, Lou tugs on her Blink-182 t-shirt, "Not going to lie, this normally does the trick."

Pushing down the tinge of jealousy in my gut, I spin around and give her an indignant sniff, "You said I get to pick what you wear tonight *and* do your hair. Now, answer the question please."

"Fine." Flopping back on the bed, Lou stares up at the mis-coloured splotches on my ceiling. I don't know where they came from, and frankly, I hope I never do. First-year dorms have a lot of things going for them, but cleanliness and spaciousness are not some of them.

"I mean, we don't know how long this party is going to be, and I don't want him to suffer... so the second one?" Choosing to ignore the uncertainty pinned to the end of that sentence, I resume my hunt until I find what I'm looking for.

"Aha!" Using my weight to force the rickety closet door wider, I reach for the back of my closet and pull out a cobalt blue, low-cut top I have been saving for an occasion such as this one.

Truth is, half the clothes in here are things I have picked up for my roommate and I just keep them safe until outings call for them to be revealed. Not that Lou knows that, of course, I let her think she's borrowing something of mine, and always end up letting her keep it.

It sounds worse than it is. I like to think of it as investing in my roommate's wellbeing. Everything I buy for Lou always looks amazing on her, but if I gave her everything at once, she'd be overwhelmed. Plus, Lou is blessed with modest curves and a slight frame that she keeps hidden under baggy clothes, so I consider it my responsibility to help show off the amazing figure Lou doesn't even realize she has.

The only reason she hasn't caught on to my scheme yet is because the poor girl doesn't have a clue how sizing works.

"I've never worn a backless shirt before." Holding up the shirt backwards, Lou peers at it like it's a puzzle she can't figure out.

Walking the two steps from my closet to my bed, I gently take the shirt from Lou's hands and turn it around to explain the item's function.

"My dear Lou, you aren't ready for a backless top. That would mean no bra." The look of horror on my non fashionista's face has me patting her hand in reassurance.

"This is the front. It's meant to show off those impressive boobs you have."

"That's the *front?*" Disbelief oozes through her tone as I nod my head patiently.

"That's right. Remember the movie we watched last night? Bend and snap? This is how to show off your snap without breaking Wes' nose."

I love my roommate dearly, but I wouldn't put it past her to accidentally put her boyfriend in the emergency room. The pair of them met crashing into each other on move-in day, so pulling a Paulette from *Legally Blonde* really isn't that far of a stretch.

"The colour is going to look amazing with your eyes, especially once I add some sparkly powder and do your hair." I clap my hands with finality, leaving no room for argument.

"Wes does love my eyes." Murmuring the words almost unconsciously, Lou continues to analyze the piece of fabric taunting her on the bed. Satisfied my job is complete, I walk back to my closet and start rummaging for myself.

"What are you going to wear tonight?" The question pulls a smile to my lips as a memory flashes behind my eyes. Closing them for the briefest second, I step back into the past only for heartache to yank me back to present.

Sparks of pain shoot up my torso, scattering like fireworks along my ribs, and sending a prick of heat behind my eyes. The phantom pain isn't anything new and neither is the wave of grief, but it still manages to throw me off-balance.

"Stella? Everything okay?"

Quickly clearing my throat, I blindly grab the first item in front of me.

"Right as rain. This is what I'm going to wear." I can't see Lou's expression from the tears blurring my eyes, but I hear her sharp intake of breath.

"Are you sure you're... oh my." The silence that follows is long enough for me to compose myself and look at the item I randomly choose from my side of the closet.

Oh, dear God.

Pasting a smile to my face, I drape the item on the bed for Lou's scrutiny. It was not at all what I had in mind for tonight, but I said I was going to wear it so that's what I am going to do.

The O'Brien stubbornness can be a real pain in the ass sometimes.

"Well?" I mentally flip through the hairstyle options I'd been considering for tonight and discard them all. This calls for something different.

A smile snakes from the corner of Lou's lips, all the way up to the tips of her ears, "Caveman Cody might find himself with harder issues to handle tonight than just his recovery."

I burst out laughing, "Wes has even turned your puns dirty, hasn't he?"

A sly grin is all I get in response.

Chapter 3

♥

Cody

"There he is!"

The living room explodes into cheers. You would think I am a long-lost soldier coming back from war, not an injured defenseman who participated in the sprint workout last week.

A lopsided orange banner hangs from a pock-marked kitchen table, and if the tedious swinging is anything to go by, the duct tape holding it in place was hastily put on just seconds before I stepped through Mason's front door.

Laughter bubbles up in my throat as I read the shaky black bubble letters decorating the sign in our school colours: *Let Cap's Alcohol Recovery Begin!*

Side hugs and back claps pull me farther into the room as familiar and unfamiliar faces swarm before me. Mason's living room is bigger than mine, but not enough to accommodate the number of people here tonight.

Taber is well-known for its small-town parties but not so much for its studious students.

Squeezing my way through the crowd, I make it to the kitchen, being careful to step around the banner made in my honour. I head straight for the stack of red solo cups sitting next to the keg and grab one just as a familiar voice rings in my ear.

"Heard Hunter took you for quite the spin last week." Waiting for my turn at the keg, I turn to see Taber's freshman goalie, Nico Montez grinning back at me.

I sigh in good nature, "And here I thought my players would wait at least two weeks before they brought up my embarrassment."

Nico laughs, the dark scruff on his jaw a stark contrast to the glistening teeth beneath, "You have too high of expectations, Cap. You should know by now no one takes the piss better than Tigers."

A smile tugs my lips, and I raise my glass in acknowledgement. With a smirk, Nico mimics the motion, tapping his plastic cup against my empty one, "We all need to be remembered for something, Cap."

Stifling a groan, I keep my smile in place as I take my turn at the keg. Besides my spectacular sprint letdown, the only other memorable thing I've done as captain is taken a beating during our season opener with Taber's rivals, Silverwood Sabers.

Our team had done well up until the last quarter, but the moment I'd pushed Hunter out of the way and gotten rundown by Vector Vin, it was all over. My team had refused to continue playing after I was shipped off to the hospital, so we had scheduled a rematch for the following weekend.

And Taber's champion lacrosse team had lost.

Badly.

Having been undefeated champions for five years in a row, the team had taken the hit hard, and it didn't help that I couldn't participate in practices until just recently. It took all of us two minutes to realize that being a captain from the sidelines was equivalent to being a lifeguard at the Olympics. Absolutely useless.

"Are you looking forward to the break?" Shuffling over to the tall Latino, I press my back into the shabby-looking pantry door as more people funnel into the kitchen for refills. Mason's place might look like a nice starter home on the outside, but on the inside, years of use have stripped it down to something that looks like a show home for tight student budgets.

My question sparks a bright smile to light up Nico's face, "Couldn't be more excited to be going home. It is my family's turn to host this year, so all my cousins will be breaking down our door."

I smile wistfully, "You have a big extended family?"

"The biggest. My parents were the only ones who stopped at one child. The rest of my aunts and uncles felt the need to re-stimulate the world population." Nico rolls his eyes, but the love shining through them tells me a different story.

"What about you? Heading back to Lethbridge after exams?"

Taking a sip of my beer to collect my thoughts, I give Nico a nonchalant shrug, "Thinking I might stay here. Catch up on recovery and all that. My pride can only let Hunter beat me so many times." The rookie laughs just as his phone dings.

"Sorry, it's Wes. One sec." Waving him away, I take another sip of my beer and survey the room. My eyes are accustomed to picking out Stella's unnatural shade of platinum in a crowd, so it doesn't take me long to determine she hasn't arrived yet. Come to think of it, I haven't seen Wes or his girlfriend tonight either.

I frown, rescanning the room, and spot Nico still talking on his phone. The sleek black dress shirt he's sporting tonight shifts against his torso as Nico rapidly shakes his head at whatever is being said down the line. Unease pricks my stomach as I picture the hunk of metal Wes drives, one that barely qualifies as a working vehicle. The grip on my solo cup tightens as images of car wrecks flash through my mind, every worst-case scenario arriving at one common denominator.

Stella could be in trouble.

Stella could be *hurt*.

Full-blown panic thunders through my veins as I start making my way over to Nico. I'm about five feet from my destination when a slurring voice shouts for my attention.

"Cap! Come show these rookies how it's done."

I look over my shoulder to see Mason, the host and graduating defenseman this year, lounging on the couch with a pretty brunette draped over him. The combination of the girl's green dress and Mason's ginger complexion immediately paints them as the most festive couple in the room.

My eyes skip to the drunken oval slowly forming around the senior defenseman and it takes me a moment to realize they are all holding cards.

Anxiety continues to itch beneath my skin as I glance back to Nico, who is no longer on the phone and is making his way over to the card game. I exhale heavily, looking down at the sticky laminate flooring beneath my sneakers, and will my stress levels to climb back down.

If Nico isn't worried about his best friend or the passengers then I shouldn't be either.

Chugging the rest of my drink, I go for a quick refill before joining my teammates on the floor. Someone passes me a deck of cards and I shake out my suddenly shaky hands.

"Y'alright there, Cap?"

I start to slowly shuffle the cards before responding, "Never better. Now, does everyone know how to play hearts?"

A drunken chorus of *I think so* goes around and I deal out the cards, choosing to ignore the game my own heart seems to be playing lately.

"Son of a bitch!" Hunter's exclamation has me leaning into the person on my left as laughter takes over my body. I am well into my buzz now and beating Hunter in cards is the yummiest cherry on top.

Is yummiest a word? If not, it should be.

"Uh oh. I think we've got ourselves a drunk captain." Cheers erupt from the mass on the floor as Nico uses his body weight to push me back into upright position.

I frown in his general direction, certain the goalie's eyes have never been so dark before. Can irises be black or just pupils?

"I don't see you playing to win over there, Montezzz." His last name comes out in three long syllables and suddenly I'm laughing all over again.

"Here, drink this." A water bottle is pressed into my hands, and I immediately gulp it down. There were many hard lessons I had to learn in my first year, and not drinking water when it's available was one of them.

"Thank you." There are no direction to the words, but the reassuring pat on my back makes me think they arrived at the right person.

"Anytime, Cap. Don't think I've ever seen you let loose before." My head swivels towards the voice, one I have yet to hear tonight.

"Wes!" A dopey smile takes over my face as laughing green eyes come into focus. "It's *so* good to see you. What took you so long?"

Chuckling, Wes rakes a hand through his dark hair, drawing my attention to the Metallica shirt my favourite rookie is wearing tonight. Wes is more of a Disney soundtrack than a head-banging rock n' roll kind of guy, so the new attire must be for the new Mrs.

"Aw, I missed you too. We had some trouble starting my car, so we did a bit of a switcheroo." Dropping into a crouch next to me on the floor, Wes throws an arm around my shoulders and pulls me close enough to question both his relationship status and his sexuality.

The guys sitting around us don't even bat an eye, which says a lot about Wes' presence on the team.

"Switcheroo?" The man-sized lapdog finally leans far enough away that my personal bubble begins to reform. Brushing off a piece of invisible lint on his shirt, Wes makes himself comfortable beside me, spreading his jean-clad legs out on the floor in front of him.

"Mm, we ended up driving Stella's car." His eyes do a sweep of the room, and I can tell the moment they land on Lou because his lips pull into an easy, content smile.

The beer buzz I was cherishing earlier pales in comparison to the anticipation building up inside me. Unable to help myself, I do an obvious scope of the room, head swivelling from side-to-side until my sight zeros in on the person I have been waiting all night for.

Wow.

My mouth goes dry as I take in the vision in front of me, my heart audibly thumping against my chest.

"Your tongue is hanging out." Nico murmurs the words as he deals out the next round.

I snap my mouth shut, struggling to tear my gaze away from the toned legs peeking out from the incredibly short dress Stella is wearing tonight. She shifts just as I'm about to return to the game and suddenly I get a clear shot of who she's talking to.

A sound rips from my throat and to my horror, I realize it's a growl. I blame the alcohol.

Stella

This dress is fucking tight.

I was surprised I managed to get it on, but even more surprised when the seams didn't burst the minute I sat in Wes' car. Either Lady Luck is on my side tonight or this dress was made by a seriously impressive seamstress.

At this point, I wouldn't be surprised if it was a bit of both.

"So, you live on campus?" I try not to roll my eyes at Hunter's obvious leering but it's getting old fast. Once Lou gave Wes the okay to make his rounds, this rookie decided to make his move.

Let me be the one to say, thus far, his performance has been seriously subpar.

Lou, the friendly one of our pair, shakes her head patiently, "We met on the first day of university. We're roommates."

Hunter flicks his eyes to Lou but before his gaze can drop below her chin, he nervously glances back to the living room where Wes' animated voice can be heard. I bite back a laugh as Hunter visibly accepts defeat and steers his gaze away from the slope of Lou's popping cleavage and back onto friendly territory with my girl's beautifully made-up face.

As I'd predicted, the cobalt blue top not only accentuates Lou's modest curves but also brings out the different shades of grey swirling around her pupils. With the tiniest touch of blue eyeshadow and some sparkles for her collarbones, Lou catches the attention of every male in this room.

Unfortunately, the lacrosse player currently taking too much of my personal space is ruining the first ten minutes of this party. Hunter's millennial, shaggy, teen idol hair leaves much to be desired, and we aren't even going to mention the unsubtle bicep flex he did while handing me a drink.

I can't believe I made out with this guy.

Tugging at the ends of his Flames jersey, Hunter takes a step closer to me. "That's sweet. I room with a couple of teammates on campus as well."

His hand not holding the solo cup snakes towards me, and I resist the urge to smack it away. Why guys think one make out means they can touch you whenever they want is something I will never understand.

"Bet it's not even a ten-minute walk from my dorm to yours. Gotta love convenience, eh?" The wink Hunter throws my way is almost as smarmy as his smile. I return it without hesitation, keeping one eye on the hand closing in on my waist.

"That must mean you live in the same building as Wes. Last I heard, he was pretty protective of the people his girlfriend hangs out with." My smile widens until I feel my canines pop out. His hand stills, midair, ten centimeters from my body.

"So, I guess that means he knows exactly where to find you if you crossed a line he didn't like." The hand starts to backtrack as I continue with an air of casualty, "But the good news is Wes doesn't have many friends who would help hide a body. Isn't that right, Lou?"

In my peripheral, I see Lou clamping her teeth down, trying not to laugh.

"Oh, wait." I tap on my chin with false realization, "Wes is friends with *everybody*." I let out a laugh that would make Tinker Bell stash every ounce of pixie dust she owns and quiver with fear.

"So where does that leave you, Hunter?"

"I-I need to go." The rookie doesn't even say goodbye as he turns on his heel and stumbles through the mass of people, trying to put as much space between us as possible.

Smart man.

Lou snorts into her drink, shaking her head, "The poor guy will never approach you again."

"Only if I'm lucky." I smile and toss a carefully crafted curl over my shoulder.

It took me over an hour to curl every strand of my waist-length, pin-straight hair, but the finished result was well worth the effort. The platinum curls create the perfect backlash for the short, *tight*, halter dress I accidentally chose to wear tonight. I finished the look off with a touch of navy eyeliner and voilà! Three hours later, I was ready to party.

If there's one motto I've created all on my own, it's that perfection takes time.

"Trip! I need your help." Wes' voice breaks through the thumping bass and Lou looks at me with wide eyes.

"Ten bucks says Nico dealt him a bad hand."

I burst out laughing and hold out my hand, "Twenty says he got a good hand but doesn't know it."

Lou smirks and grabs my hand, "Deal."

She starts to make her way towards the cramped living room, and it takes all of two seconds for her to realize I'm not following. Pausing right before the dense crowd swallows her up, Lou looks back with concern, "Stella?"

I hold up the drink in my hand and tilt my head towards the kitchen, "I need to pour this out. I'll catch you in a bit, okay?"

A worry line appears between Lou's perfectly penciled brows – done by yours, truly – so I hold up my phone and tap it in reassurance. With a hesitant nod, Lou resumes her trek through the drunken wilderness, and I wait until I hear Wes' excited exclamation about her arrival before heading the other way.

One glance at the overcrowded kitchen full of splashing drinks and rambunctious laughter is all the motivation I need to change course and head down the hallway in search of a bathroom. Thankfully, it's still early at the party scene, so the number of couples groping against the wall are few and far between.

I duck past a doorframe that's missing a door and come to a mud room. A satisfied smile hits my face when I spy the bathroom tucked into the far corner, the door left ajar so I can see the mirror peeking through the doorway.

Bickering voices hit my ears before my eyes register the figures in the mirror. The back of Hunter's mop-like haircut gives him away immediately, but his ridiculously huge hockey jersey blocks whoever is facing him. The murmurs are too low for me to make out what's being said, but loud enough for me to distinguish the tone is nothing short of furious.

Patiently leaning against the wall for the couple to wrap up their argument, I take a moment to study the dark liquid swirling inside my cup. The white plastic brings out the brown pigment in the beer, and I take a cautious sniff.

Disgusting.

Faint tremors trickle up my left side, a constant reminder of why I avoid this stuff. Beer. Alcohol. Substances that can impair judgement. Because at the end of the day it's all fun and games until someone gets hurt. Or someone ends up dead.

Or, in my case, both.

Pressing a hand against my side, the thick veins of my scar bulge up to meet my hand. If only memories could be washed away as easily as the beer in my cup.

A crash in the bathroom causes me to jump, and I look up to see Hunter storming back to wherever he came from. I hurry to help whoever got left behind and crash into the victim making his way out of the bathroom.

With a scream, I topple headfirst towards the toilet. Right before I can make contact with the porcelain bowl, steady hands reach out and halt my momentum. The calluses on said hands are rough against my skin and it takes all my will power not to sigh and lean further into the brick wall that saved me.

I know without looking up exactly who it is. I've seen these calluses get made day-after-day in the gym each morning.

"Better be careful there, Stel. Next time I might not be there to catch you."

I scoff, taking a step away and breaking our embrace, "Please. We both know I do the heavy lifting around here."

Cody lets out a laugh and crosses his arms in mock defence. The black t-shirt he's wearing is nothing fancy but the way it pulls tight against his biceps is a trick Hunter should learn how to do.

I take in the familiar figure in front of me, the impossibly wide shoulders, the annoyingly sharp jawline that only softens on the rarest of occasions. Cody's signature blonde fauxhawk stands tall and proud, giving him a couple of extra inches to his modest height. Not that Cody needs the extra inches, the guy is built like a brick shithouse.

He grins, "Guess it's a good thing I'm allowed to lift again."

Butterflies I choose to ignore take flight in my stomach as I put a fist on my hip and cock it out in challenge, "But you haven't been lifting recently, now, have you?"

Dragging his gaze from the top of my head down to my argument-ready toes, Cody takes his sweet time bringing his molten brown eyes back up to mine.

"I got cleared to start tomorrow." Oh.

My posture must reflect my defeat because a quirk of an eyebrow has Cody taking a confident step towards me.

"Noticed I've been away, hmm?" A trace of beer stains his breath but for some reason it no longer smells like the unappealing, murky liquid in my glass.

It smells like something I want to taste.

I feign disinterest, turning my back to him as I dump the beer down the sink and rinse out the plastic cup, "Honestly, I was more worried about your gains. You've probably lost them all by now."

Turning around, I bite back a gasp. I hadn't heard the varsity captain move, but somehow, he managed to sneak up behind me so now I am almost plastered against his chest.

Carefully placing both hands on the sink behind me, Cody lowers himself down until we are face-to-face, and I'm caged between his muscular arms. He manages to do the whole move without touching a single hair on my body, managing to stay respectful in the most dominating way possible.

I hate how much I love it.

"You aren't wrong about that one." With our faces level, I can see the alcohol glaze in his eyes. There's something else swirling around in there but my focus is too centred on my erratic breathing to figure out what it could be.

"Well, what are you going to do about it?" The question comes out breathier than I intended, and I mentally scold my feminine urges for succumbing to such a blatant alpha move.

My hormones are stronger than that.

He holds my gaze for a painstakingly long second then starts closing the space between us. My beath catches, thinking he's about to kiss me, but at the last second, Cody swerves like the talented lacrosse player he is and whispers softly in my ear, "We can start rebuilding tomorrow morning. Same time, same place."

He straightens and gives me the nod we've exchanged every morning for the past four months. "You know where to find me."

"You better not be late because you're hungover!" I shout the words to his retreating form, mentally checking off another Cody conversation victory. He might have gotten the drop on me tonight with the drunken alpha moves, but I got the last word.

Grinning in triumph, I start humming One Direction as I fix the few curls that fell astray. I'm just finishing up when a fading voice reaches my ear, so faint I almost wonder if I imagined it.

"I won't be late, Stel. You're in my calendar."

The grin leaves my lips as my mental tally drops to zero.

Chapter 4

♥

Cody

The fire alarm goes off beside my head.

I groan in agony, the blaring noise bringing my disoriented senses conscious as I blink up at an unfamiliar ceiling.

"Who the fuck set an alarm?"

The gravelly voice hits my ears and I shift on the couch to see Nico glaring up at me from his makeshift bed on the floor. The alarm continues to scream as I stare back, confused as to why I'm on somebody's couch and why we aren't all evacuating.

Oh, right. Mason's party.

Fingers fumbling, I search my pant pockets for my phone and squint at the time. 4:45am.

Shutting off the alarm, I swallow the nausea climbing in my throat and haul my ass off the couch. Pieces of the night before start to filter through as I stumble through the darkened hallway to the bathroom.

A monster of a hangover bangs through my skull as I flick on the lights, my bloodshot eyes and dishevelled clothes staring wearily back at myself in the mirror.

I look like shit.

Quickly stripping down and hopping in the shower behind me, I hiss out a breath as cold water hits my back, but I don't bother turning up the heat before hopping back out and throwing on the gym gear I'd stashed here the night before. I finish getting ready and creep back out the door, doing my best not to step on the shadowed bodies gracing Mason's living room floor.

The bitter, December air bites my skin the second I step outside, but it doesn't keep the smile from stretching across my face as one thought pounds its way through my dehydrated mind.

See Stella.

"The fallen captain has returned!" Throwing my bag in a cubby, I turn and see my old pal, Stephen manning the front desk like he always does. His dark 'fro seems longer and even more out of control than the last time I saw it, but the ridiculously cheerful grin brightening his face is the same.

"It's good to see you too, Stephen. How have things been?"

"Oh, you know. Same old, same old." He gives me a nonchalant shrug, the bright smile never once leaving his face. "I have missed watching you and O'Brien go at it, though."

I bark out a laugh, my hangover temporarily forgotten, "I've missed being your entertainment as well."

I spy Stella already setting up in her free-range section, pushing and arranging boxes and mats to fit whatever cardio horror she has planned.

"Well, I didn't say there wasn't entertainment." Pulling my eyes away from Stella's meticulous prep work, I look to see Stephen watching me closely.

"Oh yeah?"

He nods, "There's an ongoing bet on who the lucky guy will be."

Dread coils deep in my stomach as my eyes flick back to my camo-clad gym buddy. Stella catches me looking and taps her watch with an exaggerated huff that I can hear from across the room.

"Who's the lucky guy for?" Holding my breath, I throw Stella a friendly wave that I know will grate her nerves. She gives me a glare that could burn a hole through an iceberg.

"O'Brien, of course. Since you've been out of commission, the number of early morning regulars have jumped, and almost all of them have taken a turn asking out your Mrs." A dark eyebrow disappears into the chaos of curls, looking at me questioningly.

I raise a brow, giving nothing away, "Stel would kick your ass for calling her my Mrs. She doesn't belong to anybody, and she can handle herself."

Like hell she will.

I'm already formulating a plan as I give the room a sweep, assessing the new faces scattered among the first floor.

"If I were you," My focus is no longer on Stephen as I give him one last pat on the back. "I wouldn't place my bets on anyone other than Stella."

Especially if I have anything to do with it.

"Aw, you underestimate me, Cody. I'm going to win this bet. You just wait and see." Chuckling to himself, Stephen waves me away and retreats to the computer hidden behind the counter.

I take a collecting breath and wander over to my usual spot in the weight room section. The new faces regard me curiously but no one comments as I make myself comfortable on the bench press. I always use the bench tucked in the corner for a couple of reasons, one of which being the vantage point I get over the free-range section.

I wasn't lying when I said Stella can take care of herself, but it helps to know I can be there if she needs me. It's what her brother would want, and I'm not about to let him down.

Stella

When you hear the term gym buddies, most people picture two friends who hit the gym together, perform some sort of team exercise, and hold each other accountable for achieving fitness goals. That is the definition you would find on Google, and more or less the response you would get from a Canadian survey.

And yet, for Cody and me, that's not it.

We don't go to the gym together and we certainly don't work-out together either. He despises any form of cardio – yet somehow manages to run around a lacrosse field every day – while I am not the biggest fan of repetitive, heavy lifting. Cody is a typical gym buff, while I am the queen of HIIT.

I guess you could say because we are always at the gym at the same time, ergo, we are gym buddies. It doesn't make sense, but it works.

And sometimes the things you can't explain are the ones that hold the most meaning.

I wipe the sweat from my brow, chest heaving as I count down the seconds between my burpee sets. My heart felt like it was going to explode when I started my fifth round, but that doesn't stop me from finishing the next set.

Part of the process is pain. Without pain, you have no process. Without a process, you have no results. Are you about to settle for no results, Stella?

"No." I force the word out between my gritted teeth, pushing myself to do an extra two sets. There's no point in finishing a workout if you aren't going to challenge yourself. And if there's one thing my father raised me to do, it was push past limits.

I finish the second bonus round and flop to the ground in a heap. My lungs feel like they're on fire while my limbs feel shaky. I give myself a whole minute to breathe then launch into my core workout.

Once I'm satisfied every last fiber in my body has been used to the point of exhaustion, I finally call it a day. Closing the workout on my smart watch, I use the next five minutes to put everything back where I found it, using a rag to wipe away stray sweat goblets.

"You missed a spot." The voice that has been missing these last few weeks reaches my ears and I have to stop myself from squealing with joy.

Be subtle, Stella. Cool, calm, collected.

Be the cucumber.

Tucking my excitement back into the depths of my sore core, I settle for a smile that stretches from ear to ear before turning around.

Sweat glistens along Cody's forehead, his blonde fauxhawk untouched from his workout. A quick glance at the veins protruding through Cody's forearms tells me it was some sort of arm day today.

"Feel free to get it for me." I toss him the cloth and much to my amusement, he actually drops to one knee and wipes a spot on the floor.

Got to love a man who doesn't mind being on his knees.

"I could get used to this view." The innuendo slips out of my mouth and Cody's head whips in my direction.

Damn, I really thought that one was going to slide.

"Is there anything else I can do for you while I'm down here?" His response comes fast and quick, the teasing glint in his dark eyes unmistakably dirty.

I unconsciously lick my lips and his gaze drops to a spot on my chest. My breathing grows heavy as a bead of sweat drips into my sports bra.

"Wouldn't be a bad side gig, being the O'Brien's cleaner." Clearing his throat, Cody drops his gaze to the floor and pushes himself back up to standing.

The charge in the air turns from sexually charged to sexually frustrated as the varsity captain uses the same weapon of defence he uses every time something almost interesting happens between us.

"I have a feeling you're a lot cleaner than Mo." And there it is.

My big, bad brother to the rescue.

"You'd be surprised." I sigh with defeat, unsure why I still hope these interactions might steer past the flirty friend territory.

It's a dance we've been through too many times to count, and it always goes the same way: Friendly banter becomes borderline flirtatious. Topic of Mo comes up and suddenly there's an uncrossable chasm between us.

With the exception of last night, I've never seen Cody make a move. And that was probably the result of too much alcohol and not enough brain power to remember his unwavering, puppy dog loyalty to my older brother.

I sound bitter, I know, but there's really no other way to put it.

We head to the cubbies together, silently walking side-by-side. On a usual morning, we'd be bickering about some mundane topic, but I can't think of a single topic that doesn't centre on Cody's frustrating behaviour. So, I keep silent.

Which is unusual for me.

"Stella!"

I mutter a curse as Hayden comes running up behind us. He shoots Cody an ambiguous look before turning to me, "Thought I'd missed you."

I resist the urge to make a snarky comment and my sullen silence has Cody glancing over at me.

"So, I know you said you were too busy for coffee, but I was thinking if we are both here every morning anyways, what do you say we work out together? Maybe Friday?"

Hopeful blue eyes bore deep into my soul, making absolutely no dent on my Slytherin personality.

I open my mouth to say no when I spot the frown dancing across Cody's features. I pause, taking a second to relish the sight of unease staining his handsome features, and make a decision I immediately regret.

"That sounds great, Hayden. I'll see you Friday."

The line on Cody's forehead deepens and I resist the urge to celebrate. Taber's varsity captain might be good at stirring up my emotions, but this time he's the one who is going to suffer.

In the battle of the O'Brien siblings, Cody picked Mo's side, so now it's time that I picked mine.

"Awesome! Guess I'll be seeing you bright and early Friday morning." Hayden goes to throw me a wink but ends up flinching hallway through. I don't risk looking at Cody's brooding face because chances are I'll burst out laughing if I do.

"Okay, bye!" I give Hayden a flirty finger wave and head for the door. Cody keeps pace with me, his footsteps getting heavier by the step.

"I think he's pretty cute, don't you? God, I just love those freckles!" I clap my hands with excitement, barely keeping my laughter in check.

Did someone say productive gym session?

Cody grunts, "You could do better."

Casually intertwining his fingers with mine, I squeeze them reassuringly, "Hey, it's just one date. I'll be okay."

Shooting me a weary smile, Cody bumps his shoulder into mine like the friends we will always remain to be.

"You're not the one I'm worried about. You are going to eat that kid alive."

I let out a light laugh, carefully tucking my own words back into a compartment buried deep inside me.

It's just one date. You'll be okay.

Chapter 5

Cody

"Again!"

Loud curses make their way up and down the court as my players re-assemble for another round of suicides. I'm right there alongside them, doing my best to speed up recovery through stubborn will power and sheer stupidity.

Suicides hurt like hell when you're in the best of shape, never mind coming back from a cracked rib and six weeks' worth of endurance.

Sucking in a painful breath, I spit out an equally painful reminder to the team, "If it hurts, think about how much it hurt when Silverwood beat us."

Groans quickly replace the swearing, and with a blow of my whistle, we start running.

By the time the last player touches the final line, the rest of the team is collapsed on the ground, dosing each other off with water bottles. No one enjoys indoor practices but given the thirty centimeters of snow currently covering Taber's lacrosse field, there isn't much choice. Snow season came early this year so most of our fall tournaments got put on hold until the spring.

Even though we lost our undefeated title last game, it only counted as one loss under our belt, so our standing in the league was only slightly affected. The real test will be after the snow melts, when it comes down to taking home the championship banner or coming home empty handed.

"That last round was a low blow, Cap." Huffing out a laugh, Mason shakes his head and chugs the rest of his water bottle.

Wes grins, "We must have been doing a different workout because that felt like foreplay to me."

The remark sets off a round of wheezing laughter as I join the guys on the ground. With the exception of Nico, whose tanned skin seems impervious to blemishes, the rest of my players are rocking red faces and sweaty hairlines.

"Just making sure you'll miss me over the break." I steal the water bottle closest to me and take a swig. My body aches with the motion, an unsubtle reminder that my recovery isn't as complete as I'd like it to be.

Not that binge drinking on Tuesday nights is doing me any favours.

Using the corner of my shirt, I carefully wipe the perspiration lining my forehead. Nico, who is casually lounging on the gymnasium floor like he didn't just run for the last two hours, catches the motion, and lets out a wolf whistle.

"Now that is a view I'll miss over the break."

I throw him a wink and let my shirt drop. Wes snaps upright from his position on the floor and points a finger in my direction.

"See? Foreplay."

Mason chuckles, running a freckled hand through the red mop plastered against his forehead, "You guys should have seen Cap in his first year. The freshmen girls had a thing for short defensemen and would show up like groupies for every game."

Wes' jaw visibly drops as disbelieving mumbles go around the room. I'm pretty sure Hunter lets a "no way" slip out but ever since our bathroom rendezvous at the party, he's been keeping a wide berth, so it's hard to know for sure.

I hold up my hands in surrender, "The groupies weren't for me, they were for Mighty Mo. That was the year Taber broke the record for five consecutive championship wins."

Silence falls among the exhausted group, a respective silence that pays tribute to the graduated all-star and the legacy he left behind.

A legacy I've already managed to let down.

"Well, I can't wait to make it six wins this year." Wes' voice breaks through my dismal thoughts and I smile at the natural display of leadership.

"Hell yeah, I'm graduating this year, so you already know the groupies will want to see me off." Mason flips his sweat-soaked hair and pulls a pose that would make Zoolander proud.

Chuckles ring out throughout the group as I clap my hands for everyone's attention, "Alright, boys. That's enough for today. Next practice is optional, so if I don't see you, I hope everyone has a good break."

Murmurs of acknowledgment go around as my players heave themselves off the ground and head towards the changerooms.

I wait until the last player leaves the gym before turning off the gymnasium lights and following the departing mass. Taber's fitness facilities are all interconnected, so the march to the men's locker room takes less than thirty seconds before the steam of showers hit me.

As one of Alberta's smaller universities, the varsity changerooms aren't anything to brag about, they are the same size as the school's public changerooms, which is to say, long, narrow, and borderline claustrophobic.

I guess one thing the varsity side has that the public doesn't is actual shower stalls instead of communal. That being said, the four sad-looking stalls are only separated by sheet-thin curtains that are mostly see-through, so I'm not sure we are doing any better in terms of public nudity.

"I heard a rumour yesterday, Cap." Rummaging around his locker, Wes digs out the shirt he's looking for and turns to me with a grin that immediately raises my suspicions.

"Mm?" I flick a glance at the cut rookie, whose six-pack has slowly gotten more defined over the course of the season. My players might hate the cardio elements I incorporate into our training programs, but they certainly get the results.

"Trip mentioned something about Stella going on a date Friday?" Wes pauses for dramatic effect, "At the same time and location you two always work out at?"

I step into my jeans and yank them up over my waist. Hunter is in the corner, quietly listening to the conversation and wisely choosing to keep his mouth shut.

"You heard correctly." The bite in my tone has a freshly showered, towel-clad Nico pausing mid-step to survey the scene. He takes one glance at my tight posture and glances back at his best friend.

"Stella?"

Wes smirks, tugging a shirt over his head, "O'Brien found herself a new gym buddy."

Nico lets out a low whistle and I feel a muscle pop in my jaw.

"Does the fresh meat know what he's in for?" The lean Latino jerks his head in my direction, "If Cap can't keep up with the girl, I doubt some newbie is going to last long."

Wes nods in agreement, "If Stella gets to lead the workout, the dude's toast. I can't picture her taking it easy for some guy."

"Well, unless she *really* likes him. Then I could see it." Nico unhelpfully throws in a wink with the comment and I flip him off.

"It's just one date. I'm sure Stel won't go in with guns blazing." The words pass my lips and suddenly the beginning of an idea begins to take form.

A wonderful, truly awful idea.

Wes catches the Grinch-like smile taking over my features and does a double take.

"Uh oh. Nico, have you ever seen that look on Cap before?"

The freshman goalie drops his towel before moving closer to analyze my expression.

"You couldn't have held on to the towel for another minute?" I uncomfortably shift from side to side, trying to look anywhere but my rookie's package.

Which is right in front of me.

Wes lets out a laugh, "Don't worry, Cap. You'll get used to it."

I shoot him a warning look before Nico finally nods, "He looks like a man with a plan. And you're welcome."

My eyes twitch from the effort of not looking down.

"You're welcome?"

Nico gives me a modest shrug before turning and grabbing his briefs from the bench. I breathe out a sigh of relief.

I'll take a lunar eclipse over the front view any day.

"For showing you what evolution has done for mankind."

Stella

"Wait. So, let me get this straight: you agreed to work out with a guy? Who you've never met before?"

I nod in response to Lou's questions.

"But... why?"

I go to nod my head and then stop, realizing this one needs more than a yes or no answer. I open my mouth but find myself at a loss of words.

Why did I agree to work out with Hayden tomorrow morning? The answer is so simple yet feels infinitely more complicated.

Seems to be a life theme of mine.

"To get back at Cody." I cringe at the juvenile word choice, but it's the barren truth. And ever since Lou and I hit a rocky patch in our friendship because I refused to open up, I figure it's best to go with the most direct route possible.

The hand stabbing the cafeteria's poutine stalls at my confession. I can practically hear the wheels of my roommate's brain turning overtime.

"Because he didn't let you visit him at the hospital? I thought we were over that." I bristle at the comment, a topic that's still sore but one I have exhausted on too many occasions.

I'm not one who easily admits I was in the wrong, but even I can't deny there was a rough adjustment period during Cody's recovery. I went from furious to furiously disappointed as the injured defenseman's hospital stay prolonged for what seemed like an indefinite amount of time. His overall lack of communication told me all there is to know on his perspective of our friendship, but it still hurt to hear about Wes' ER visits and no mention of Cody wanting to see me.

He was suffering from severe internal injuries. But still. A text or something would have been nice.

Needless to say, that issue was raised weeks ago and no longer applies to the situation at hand. Because six weeks ago, Cody would never have hit on me at a house party. He would never have almost kissed me. And he most certainly would never have shown the slightest inclination of being jealous.

Over-protective, maybe. But not jealous.

"It's not about the hospital visitations. He just seemed angry to know there might be someone else I'm willing to go to the gym with."

Which is ridiculous because as we've gone over, Cody and I don't even go to the gym together, we are just there at the same time.

Is anyone else starting to see the problem here?

A glint of understanding lights up Lou's grey eyes, "Oh, so you're trying to make him jealous."

"No, not jealous. More like... unstable." I flick the end of my French braid over my shoulder and give my roommate a beaming smile.

"Unstable." Disbelief echoes in Lou's tone, but I choose to ignore it.

"That's right. Plus, it's always good to mix things up once in a while." A smirk tugs the corner of Lou's mouth, but I choose to ignore that as well.

"You are the queen of routine, Stella. I don't think I've seen you eat a dinner that doesn't consist of grilled chicken and spinach."

I shrug, completely oblivious to whatever she's implying, "That's called consistent eating. *Healthy,* consistent eating." I give her container of poutine a meaningful look and get a fry thrown in my direction.

"Okay, Miss Denial. So, what's your plan?"

"Plan?"

Lou rolls her eyes, using her fork to scoop up a cheese curd from the steaming pile of fries and gravy.

"Your game plan. For the date. Are you going to make Hayden do one of your cardio circuits?"

I hum to myself, going over the various scenarios in my mind. Almost all of them ends with Hayden never talking to me again or Stephen having to carry him out on a stretcher. Which doesn't sound half bad, but sort of defeats the purpose.

"That would be mean spirited. I'll just let him lead the workout."

Lou nods thoughtfully, "Probably the safest route."

I hold up my hand for a high five, but Lou just looks at me wearily. I settle for a gentle fist bump against her hand and give her a reassuring smile.

"It's going to be great, Lou. Just wait and see."

Who I was trying to convince with that statement, I couldn't tell you.

Chapter 6

♥

Stella

The scream fills my ears and I wake up with a gasp.

I sit up in bed, gulping down oxygen like I'm a sailor drowning at sea. Heart racing, I stay panting in bed for a good five minutes before rolling over and checking the time.

4:15am. Right on time.

Swinging my legs off the bed, I walk the four steps to my door and flick on the light. My face looks drawn and weary, my eyes bloodshot with dark bags seeping beneath them. The only thing that remains intact after a long, restless night is my loose platinum braid, and even that looks flatter than usual.

I turn off the alarm I've yet to need these past two years and start prepping for the day. I only use the bare makeup essentials for the gym, that is to say, a heavy dose of concealer and four swipes of mascara.

My mother always told me there was no reason for anyone to not look put together and that's something that has always stayed with me.

I made sure to lay out today's gym clothes last night, so it doesn't take me long to get ready. Pulling up my hair into a top knot, I secure it with two elastics, having long since learned one doesn't hold out too well when I'm doing any sort of jumping exercise.

I pause in front of the bathroom mirror on my way out the door, pulling up my tank top like I do every morning. Everyone's torso is divided into sections, but mine more than most. Hard earned abs pop over the top of my waistband but it's not the muscles I take time to study every morning.

The jagged edge of my scar burns a trail up my right side, the thick white line jutting out from the soft patch of skin that goes from my waist to my ribcage. From there, the marred skin becomes more than just a single line, it becomes an intricate web of scar tissue that dances unevenly along my ribs before seeking shelter in the confines of my sports bra.

I inhale deeply, watching my breath push against the taught, damaged skin.

Healing is such a funny thing. It's a miracle on all accounts but even the toughest cells can never return to what they once were. Rough, ugly skin tissue replaces what was once innocent and pure, turning something soft and beautiful into a hardened, hollow shell of what once was.

Something dangerously close to tears start to prick my eyes, so I turn my attention away from the broken side and on to the one that survived. Bold, tattooed letters stare back at my reflection before I let my top fall back down and head out the door.

On the day of the accident, I broke five ribs and lost eighteen-stitches worth of skin. It only took six weeks for my ribs to heal and for the thick tissue of my scar to pull my torso back together. The doctors were impressed by my fast recovery, but they hadn't peeked behind the outer layers.

They hadn't seen the untreated wound beating with what was left of my heart.

They hadn't seen the untreated wound beating with what was left of my heart.

My spirits begin to lift the second I step through the gym entrance. The florescent lights are almost blinding this early in the morning, the lingering scent of sweat and metal almost sickening.

And yet, I wouldn't trade it for the world.

For once, Cody is first to the gym and is waiting for me by the cubbies. He pounces on me before I have the chance to take out my indoor runners.

"So, I was thinking…"

"Sounds like a dangerous hobby." He ignores the retort, running a hand through his spiked hair and drawing my attention to the loose muscle shirt doing a poor job of covering Cody's impressive arms.

"If you need a cop-out, just send me a signal and I'll come up with an emergency to bail you out."

Busy trying to peek past the edges of his shirt for a nip slip, it takes a moment for his words to register.

"I'm sorry, what?"

Cody's eyes flick to mine, and he gives me an understanding shrug, "I overheard Hayden talking in the changeroom. Guy is planning on putting you through your paces."

My mouth drops open as my brain grinds to a stuttering halt. An indignant rage sparks inside me as I struggle to think of an appropriate response.

Finally, I manage to spit out, "*He* is going to put *me* through a fitness test?"

Cody nods, oblivious to the competitive fire smouldering from my every pore.

"He was chatting to a friend about an insane cardio workout he has planned. Was worried your little frame wouldn't be able to handle it."

Insane cardio? My *little* frame?

My vision turns red and I'm a second away from blowing smoke out of my ears. Any rational thought flees my mind as my anger takes control of the wheel, cackling like a Disney villain who has two loyal henchmen on her payroll.

I start mentally flipping through my workouts, discarding anything reasonably close to challenging. If Hayden wants to put my little frame through its paces, then I'll pick a workout that puts my body to the test.

And if he can't keep up, well, I guess we can call this date a pass or fail evaluation.

By the time my date enters the gym, my bloodlust has dropped to a comfortable simmer. A shy smile brightens Hayden's blue eyes as he approaches me.

"Stella, hey! I was thinking about what workout we could do together-"

"I've got one planned." I cut him off before he can finish the sentence. Hayden looks taken aback by my abruptness but recovers quickly.

"Oh, okay cool. Hopefully I won't have to go too easy on you, eh?" He throws me a wink and I return it with a smile that would make wiser men run for the hills.

Unfortunately, Hayden isn't a wise man.

"Guess we'll find out." Keeping my sadistic smile in place, I give Cody a tight nod, and lead my unsuspecting victim to his final resting place.

I start humming as I lay out the mats in our free-range section, easing Hayden into a false sense of security. He hasn't stopped smiling since he got here, but that's soon about to change.

My date made an assumption, and you know how the saying goes.

Two repeating thoughts thrum though my body as I gently guide my baby calf to the slaughterhouse.

Hayden thought he could break an O'Brien.

I'm going to show him what being broken feels like.

Cody

Twelve minutes and thirteen seconds.

That's how long it took for Hayden to go running for the closest trash can.

"Aw, shit. I'm going to have to clean that up, you know." Stephen and his unruly curls materialize beside me, and I choke back a laugh.

"At least your bet is over." I tap the stopwatch app on my phone, ending the timer I'd set after watching Stella and Hayden start their workout.

"Hell, this doesn't count. That man is going to be traumatized for the rest of his life and no one else is going to have the balls to ask out O'Brien for at least six months." Stephen huffs with annoyance, giving me the evil eye.

"Don't try and pretend you didn't have anything to do with this, Ellsworth."

I smile ruefully, "I just did what needed to be done."

"What needed to be done, my ass." Shaking his head, Stephen wanders over to the garbage can Hayden has all but disappeared into.

I would be lying if I said I didn't feel a bit guilty about the situation. I may or may not have exaggerated the truth to rile Stella up a bit.

Okay, I may have exaggerated a lot.

To be fair, I didn't expect her to absolutely kill the guy. I was just hoping to stoke the fires of her competitive nature to the point where Hayden would have to tap out.

An obvious oversight on my part.

I grab my water bottle and head over to the free-range section where Stella is finishing up the round Hayden was unable to complete. I step tentatively, aware of the dangerous charge in the air. Stella's temper is like a volcano, once it's erupted, it will either fall dormant or erupt again immediately.

Makes approaching her in this state risky to say the least.

I patiently wait for her to finish her box jumps before casually clearing my throat.

"I take it the date went well?"

She scoffs, turning so I can see satisfaction brimming in her beautiful blue eyes, "He didn't even make it to halfway."

I take another step closer, testing the waters, "I would have been disappointed if he did."

My comment hits its mark and a big, bright smile takes over Stella's features.

"Want to know a secret?"

No longer afraid of Stella's fury, my feet propel themselves forward until I'm close enough to see the sweat glistening along her hairline.

"I purposefully skipped the rest intervals." Her eyes sparkle with mischief, and I press my lips together to keep from laughing.

"Doubt that would have changed the outcome."

Stella tilts her head to the side, "No, but then he might not have cracked under thirteen minutes." Her perfectly straight teeth pop out as her smile widens.

"Would have been a shame to make it a quarter of the way through."

I laugh, stealing a glance over my shoulder to where a pale and trembling Hayden is being led out the door.

"I'm not sure he's going to be up for a second date."

Stella shrugs, drawing my attention to the hard outline of her traps and the tendrils of platinum hair sticking to her damp skin.

"He failed the first test. Wasn't going to get a second date anyway."

Tearing my gaze from the smooth skin, I raise a questioning eyebrow, "Not sure anyone is going to pass the first test if it means having the stamina of a horse."

Stella waves away my concerns with a flick of her hand, "Today was an exception. I just want someone who can keep up, not necessarily be a beast in the gym."

"Pretty sure the only beast in this gym is you, Stel."

Most girls blush when you compliment their features. Stella O'Brien only gets rosy in the cheeks when you compare her to an untamed, savage animal.

"Glad *you* can see past my little frame." I wince at the words, deciding now is not the best time to expose myself for that particular comment.

"Yeah, well, hard not to when you mercilessly pummelled me outside the club last month. Those bruises took weeks to fade, you know. Had to come up with a story to tell the guys in the changeroom."

Throwing her head back, Stella lets out a laugh that has my body feeling bruised in a whole different sort of a way.

"You totally deserved it. You were an absolute ass that night."

She's not wrong. That was the infamous night Hunter permanently marked himself in my bad books. The physical intervention I imposed on their make out session was not the politest course of action, but it got the job done.

"Don't know if anyone has ever told you this, but violence is not the answer. There's this thing called conversation and it works wonders with confrontation."

Stella smirks, "Could conversation have been more appropriate than carrying me out of the club like some wannabe firefighter?"

I narrow my eyes, my people-pleasing tendencies long forgotten as I stare down the miniature firecracker in front of me.

"I performed that carry correctly, so technically I wasn't a wannabe."

Her blue eyes darken as she meets my glare in equally narrow slits, "Whatever helps you sleep at night *Caveman*."

Ah, the famous nickname. Wes and his girlfriend sure got a kick out of that one.

I open my mouth to respond when Stella reaches down to grab her water bottle. The retort quickly dies on my tongue as her tank top rides up and I get a clear shot of her left side.

"Is that a tattoo?" The question leaves my lips in shock, partly from the realization that I have never seen Stella's torso, but also because I never pinned Mo's younger sister for the type to get a tattoo.

Don't get me wrong, this isn't me being stereotypical, it's simply an observation. When it comes to gym rats there seem to be two types of people: those who see their body as a masterpiece and want to use intricate pieces of ink to display it, or those who see their body as a piece of art already and wouldn't want to cover up a single inch.

Two very different mentalities, yet both run on the same vain theme.

And that's not to say you can't be both, it's just most people who have tattoos like to show them off. And until today, I had no idea Stella might be hiding ink under her signature gym fits.

It soon becomes clear my question was not a welcome one when Stella's demeanour freezes over and she quickly tugs the ends of her top down.

"Yes, I do." Her words are clipped, making it obvious the topic is not open for discussion.

The shock must not have worn off, or maybe I'm still hungover from Tuesday, because for some reason, my mouth decides it's a good idea to pursue this conversation further.

"What is it?"

Stella levels me with a glare that could make a nation crumble to its knees. Normally, I would back off by this point, but curiosity pushes me to make another, arguably stupider inquiry, "Can I see it?"

"It's a word and no you can't." She gives me a tight nod and goes to brush past me. I grab her arm before she can make it beyond my reach.

"Hey, look at me." Reluctantly turning her head in my direction, Stella meets my gaze with a worn expression.

"I shouldn't have pried, I'm sorry."

Stella sighs with a slight shake of her head, "I got the tattoo after my mother died. It's just not something I like talking about."

I exhale heavily, immediately regretting my curiosity. I knew the O'Brien's lost their mother a couple years ago, Mo mentioned it on a few occasions. From what I can remember, it was a drunk driver who ran their mother off the road. Mo had just started university when it happened, so Stella must have been a teenager.

Gently removing my fingers from her arm, I take a step forward and wrap her into a hug. She stiffens then relaxes as I pull Stella's strong frame close to mine.

"Promise I won't be so careless next time." I whisper the words against the top of her head, the scent of her post-workout sweat filling my senses.

"Whatever, I've gotten used to your stupidity by now." Stella gives me a reassuring pat and pulls away with a smile that I know means trouble, "But I do have an idea of how you can make it up to me."

That's never a good sign.

Chapter 7

♥

Stella

"Absolutely not."

"Don't be a chicken."

"I'd rather be a chicken than wear *that*." The look of horror flashing in Cody's eyes has me biting the inside of my cheek to keep from laughing.

"You can't go two-stepping without a cowboy hat. That ruins half the fun." I wave the offensive object between us, but Cody's defensive stance doesn't move an inch.

"Two-stepping itself is bad enough. Hat hair will only make it worse."

I roll my eyes, "That's why you keep the hat on, so no one sees the disaster underneath."

You would think this man grew up in a big city, not the agriculture centre of Alberta.

Giving me the full force of his glare, Cody grabs the hat out of my hands. I squeal with excitement and quickly whip out my phone. There is no way this moment is going undocumented.

"Say, howdy!" Cody flips me the bird just as the flash goes off. I cackle with glee and stash my phone before he can even think about deleting the evidence.

Carefully adjusting the wide-brimmed hat to minimize the damage to his fauxhawk, Cody heaves a sigh, his paisley button down stretching tight against his broad shoulders.

"I can't believe you convinced me to do this."

I smirk, flipping the end of my long braid over my shoulder, "Admit it, Ellsworth. You've always wanted to dress up as a cowboy."

"I'm more of a cape and tights kind of guy."

"In that case, you're welcome for broadening your horizons." I give him a beaming smile, holding out an elbow for my cowboy escort to grab on.

Muttering under his breath, Cody links his arm through mine and together we make our way towards the entrance of the makeshift country club Taber's student union managed to construct overnight.

Although our university is small, it always does a good job of creating unique opportunities for its students. From clubs to sports teams to campus-wide events, Taber promotes an inclusive community that helps bring students together in all kinds of social settings. Even my dear Lou, who started her university journey as one of the most socially self-conscious girls I have ever met, managed to find a home here at Taber.

Well, with the help of her adorable roommate and best friend, of course.

A crooked sign screaming, *A Two-Stepping Good Time!* welcomes us as we near the entrance, nasally singing and acoustic guitar floating out of the room.

"Look! They even got a horse." I let out a laugh as we pass the cardboard cut-out, its two-dimensional nose not quite lining up with the feed bucket hanging from an equally fake outpost.

I love this event already.

Cody lets out a groan, "We're even after this, got it?"

I pat his arm absentmindedly, my hips already swaying to the country rhythm vibrating through the polished floor.

"If you perform well tonight, then yes, we are even."

Cody's brown eyes light up with amusement as he turns his gaze to the already-packed dance floor. Jean-clad couples of all shapes and sizes stomp and clap their way across the floor, belt buckles sparkling under the dimmed lighting.

"Who's our competition?"

I grin at the question, knowing Cody is already on the same page. His competitive nature compliments my own and that is part of the reason why I wanted him as a partner tonight. Well, that and I didn't have any other options that didn't include Hunter.

Curse Lou for getting a boyfriend and leaving me to fend for myself.

"Them." I point to a couple who are unmistakeably the best two-steppers on the dance floor. The girl's two red braids spin elegantly as she twirls into the open arms of her partner. The partner matches her steps with ease, his dark skin and cowboy hat a beautiful contrast to her pale one.

I sigh in admiration, taking a moment to relish the piece of art the couple is slowly creating on the dance floor.

Mom would love this.

The thought comes unexpectedly and suddenly I'm struggling against the unmistakeable burn of my tear ducts. I get so focused on blinking that I don't notice one leaks out until a callused thumb wipes my cheek gently.

"Can I do anything to help?" Cody's voice is gruffer than usual, probably because he's nervous I'm a second away from turning into a full-blown crybaby.

Forcing the past back where it belongs, I pull myself together with a snort that would make debutantes around the world cringe.

"Nope. Let's do this."

My shriek of laughter fills the air as Cody swings me from one side of his body to the other. I gasp once my feet touch the ground, barely having time to suck in a breath before the varsity captain is spinning me around again and again.

"Pause! I'm pressing the pause button." My voice comes out shaky, my stomach still not quite back on solid ground. I drop my head between my knees to stop the room from spinning, but I end up falling forward when someone bumps into me.

A second before my face makes contact with the ground, rough hands yank me upright and press me close against a hard chest.

Did someone say déjà vu because it feels like I've been here before.

I snuggle closer to the warmth radiating from Cody's body as he gently carries me to a nearby booth. My body feels disjointed as he sets me down, my head spinning while my body sags against the leather seat. A wave of motion sickness hits me, and I turn my attention to keeping the rising nausea at bay.

"You okay, Stel?" Worried brown eyes pierce my disoriented mind, the low brim of Cody's hat drawing out the shadows of his jawline.

I give him an easy smile, stomping the sickness down, "Never better. Could have given me a heads up I was partnered with the country version of Derek Hough, though."

Cody's wry grin draws my eyes down to his lips and suddenly my stomach is clenching for an entirely different reason.

"I'm going to pretend I know who that is and say thank you."

I huff out a laugh then groan as another wave hits me. Clamping my lips together to keep from spewing my dinner all over the booth, I go back to deep breathing.

"If I'd known you get motion sick, I wouldn't have added that extra spin." Concern etches itself across Cody's face and I sigh in acknowledgement.

The O'Brien genes leave a lot to be desired in that particular department.

"Worth it. We definitely won." I whisper the words, trying to keep my lips pressed as tightly together as possible. Nothing kills the mood faster than stomach compost.

Cody chuckles and shakes his head, "Always a competition with you, isn't it?"

I shrug, not bothering to deny it. If there's one thing I've learned from my brother, it's how to be the best. And sometimes that means going for the kill even when there's nothing at stake.

The moment you let yourself off the hook is the moment your opponent will steal the spot.

You're only as good as your biggest failure, Stella.

"I'm going to get you some water. I'll be right back." I blink and suddenly Cody is gone from the booth, his jean-clad ass disappearing into the throng of cowboys mingling around Taber's paper-thin western saloon.

I take the second to look around, noting the printed out wanted posters of ancient convicts decorating the walls. My lips tug into a smile as I catch sight of the far corner closest to the bar, where drunks can pay a dollar to use a makeshift lasso to rope in the two-dimensional cattle lining the back wall. Based on the rowdy shouts coming from that section, I'd say the student body has some work to do in terms of eye-hand coordination.

"Mind if we join you?" The couple from earlier, aka our biggest competitors, casually gesture to the empty seat across from me.

Nausea momentarily forgotten, I straighten up and wave for them to sit down. "Of course! Please make yourselves comfortable."

"Thank you so much." Breathing a sigh of relief, the pretty red-head slides smoothly into the booth and her partner takes the spot beside her. The handsome black man passes his dance partner a hand-kerchief from his pocket, and she accepts it with a smile of thanks.

I watch the exchange with a drop of envy, the couple's cuteness reminding me of my own, sad single status.

"How did you two meet?" The question comes out instinctively, the gaping hole in my love life driving me to fill the void.

"Well, it's sort of a long story..." The girl breaks off with a shy laugh and the guy raises an eyebrow. "Don't look at me like that, Jamar. You tell the story if it's not that long."

Jamar shakes his head at me, "You would think it was this compli-cated journey the way Keegan tells it."

Keegan rolls her eyes, "Go on then, Romeo. Show me how its done."

Jamar throws her a wink before turning his attention back to me. The chemistry between the pair reminds me of Wes and Lou, two forces of nature driven together by some inexplicable destiny.

"It all began back in sixth grade, when this girl with beautiful red hair walked into the lunch room and stole my favourite snack."

Keegan lets out a groan, "When will those Dino gummies stop coming back to haunt me."

I laugh while Jamar shoots her a look for the interruption.

"Sorry, sorry, please continue." Toying with the end of her braids, Keegan returns the look with a sheepish smile.

Jamar sighs, "That is the first of many interruptions, I'm afraid." Taking a moment to fix his cowboy hat, Jamar shoots me an apologetic glance.

"Are you sure you want to hear this?"

I lean forward, butt cheeks already perched on the edge of the booth, "Absolutely. Tell me everything."

If I can't get my own happy ending, I may as well enjoy someone else's.

Cody

I leave Stella for two minutes and she's already filled our booth with new friends.

Carefully placing the water glass on the table, I look to see the couple we tried to out dance occupying the booth across from us. The sequins on Stella's jeans sparkle as she shifts further down the seat, her red cowgirl boots looking like something out of a bad 80s movie.

"... and it was only when I bought her mom flowers that Keegan finally confessed she liked me too."

The redhead rolls her eyes with a huff, "You forgot to mention *you* were the one who insisted we keep things casual."

"Did not."

"Did too."

I clear my throat as the couple falls into a glaring contest and look to Stella for clarification.

She lifts her shoulder in a delicate shrug, "I asked for Keegan and Jamar's origin story, but we've arrived at a standoff."

Stella's dark blue eyes dance between the pair sitting across from us, neither of them backing down. I take the chance to study her side profile, her proud chin and pert nose drawing my attention to the shimmery powder dusted along her cheekbones. There's yet to be an occasion where Stella doesn't sparkle and yet she always puts in the effort to go just that little bit further.

"What about you two? How did you meet?"

I jolt at the deep voice, forgetting we were no longer at an empty booth. Stella blinks in surprise, the edges of her pink lips tugging downwards at the corners.

The sight of her frown pulls at something deep in my gut and before I know it, I've gone and opened my mouth.

"At the gym."

Stella's eyebrows shoot up past the brim of her hat and I see her eyes widening in shock. Her frown has all but disappeared, taking the ache in my chest with it.

I throw her a wink as if to say, *play along.*

"I watched her destroy this freshman at the gym and I was hooked. As soon as his head disappeared into the garbage can, I knew I had to make my move."

Stella's lips start to twitch, and I have to talk myself down from doing a fist pump. Keegan, meanwhile, looks like she may have developed a girl crush.

"You made a guy puke at the gym? That's incredible."

Jamar shoots his girlfriend a concerned glance, "Don't get any ideas."

Stella laughs, "I don't normally make it a habit to break people, but this guy got under my skin." Scooting a little bit closer, Stella flutters her eyelashes in my direction, "Little did I know this one would *stay* under my skin."

Ignoring the warning bells going off in my head, I throw an arm around my mentor's younger sister and tug her close to me.

"What can I say? I'm a sucker for punishing blondes."

Stella's muscular frame leans into mine, the warmth radiating off her body making it hard to breathe. If I lowered my head just a couple inches my lips would be level with hers.

"Mm, and I just love a man who wears a cowboy hat."

My laugh rumbles through us both, making me hyperaware of every point of contact between us.

Shoulder. Hip. Thigh.

Keegan shakes her head with a sigh, "I always tell Jamar he should wear his more often, but he just complains it ruins his hair."

Forcing my mind from forbidden gutters, I look across the table and exchange a supportive glance with the man who understands my pain.

Stella huffs, her exaggerated breath pressing her body tighter against mine.

"Men."

Keegan pretends to clink an imaginary glass against Stella's untouched water on the table. Jamar groans good-naturally and steals a glance at his watch.

"Well, as much as I love girl-bonding over male flaws, I think it's time for us to go. We've got a long night ahead of us." Jamar gives

Keegan a knowing look and the one she returns leaves no question as to what type of night lies ahead for the couple.

"Right. Lots of things to do back in our... house." With an unsubtle wink at Stella, Keegan holds out her hand for a shake, "But it was so lovely meeting you. You'll have to teach me your cardio secrets so I can give this one a run for his money."

Jamar slides out of the booth with a sigh, "Here we go again."

Stella jumps up and bends over the table to latch on to Keegan's hand. I try my best not to look, I really do, but the sequins glittering along Stella's ass draw my attention like I'm a gemologist who specials in bedazzled jeans.

"It would be my pleasure! Take care guys."

She plops herself back down and I bite back a sigh of relief. My own jeans are tighter than they were a minute ago but looser than they would have been if she'd stayed in that position for any longer.

The handsome couple give us one final wave then disappear into the crowd.

"They are totally going home to fuck."

I groan at Stella's comment, my mind and southern regions veer back into dangerous territory.

"Don't be crude, O'Brien."

"What? It's true." Bringing her long braid back over her shoulder, I watch as she tugs the elastic from the end and slowly starts unwinding the knots out of her hair.

"They plan to fuck all night long." Stella sings the words as her fingers make quick work of the braid, silky platinum strands falling loose with the process. She wiggles her eyebrows at me, "Should we place bets on who's going to be on top?"

I should have bought a beer when I had the chance.

"No, but I think it's time we took you home to bed."

Immediately regretting my word choice, I avoid Stella's laughing gaze as I slide out the booth and hold out my hand for her. She takes it, callused fingers rough against my own, and doesn't bother hiding the smirk taking over her face.

"What position would you like tonight, Captain? I've always wanted to save a horse."

The unspoken *ride a cowboy* hangs in the air between us, a challenge that's as tempting as the hunger glinting in her dark blue eyes. Stella's testing me and damn it if I don't want to deliver the way she wants me to.

The way *I* want to.

"Don't think my hair would make it to morning." I take the easy way out, skimming the edges of our complicated relationship without showing my cards.

Stella snorts, seeming unfazed by my subtle rejection, "Your hair wouldn't be the only thing that doesn't make it to morning."

At this point, I'm not going to make it to the end of the night.

Chapter 8

♥

Stella

I shiver as we push through Taber's main entrance, the cold night air biting through my thin jean jacket. Not my best weather choice by any means, but the denim-on-denim look was worth it.

"Why didn't you bring a real coat, Stel? There was a coat check for a reason."

Cody breaks our hand hold to shrug off his winter jacket and wrap it around my shoulders. The worn fleece sleeves hang past my hands, enveloping me in Cody's leftover body heat. I snuggle deeper into the warmth, not bothering to protest the act of chivalry.

"Because I knew you'd bring one for me."

Cody grunts, his breath visible against the dark night sky.

I fall silent, tilting my head back to spy the faint stars shining above us. It's easy to spot the one that shines the brightest, just left of the crescent moon peeping through the clouds. I sneak a look at Cody then blow a quick kiss to the star, a tradition my mom and I created back when she was alive, and we'd had a really good day.

The more love you give, the more you'll get. Which star are you going to choose tonight my darling girl?

I smile at the memory, it's one I haven't had in years. If there was one thing my mother believed in, it was that the universe provides if you're willing to give something in return. For her, that meant spending every day of her life performing little acts of kindness to anyone and everyone that crossed her path. Whether that meant donating her last dollar or being the first to raise a toast, my mother was the brightest star long before her soul drifted into the night sky.

"I, uh, had a good time tonight." Cody's gravelly voice drags me back to present and I turn to see his wind-bitten cheeks smiling sheepishly at me.

"Oh, did you now?" Despite my teasing tone, a beaming smile takes over my features.

I've never had a good poker face.

He nods, deadpan, "Not the worst Friday night I've had."

I throw my head back and laugh, the freezing wind picking up the sound and carrying it far away. Snow crunches under our boots as we approach the doors to my residence building, and with a quick swipe of my access card, I lead us inside.

"Thank you for tonight, Cody. I mean it." My voice sounds louder now that we're inside and a glimpse of my reflection in the night-painted window has me holding back a wince.

Alberta winds are *such* a bitch.

Cody crosses his arms and leans against the corridor wall, the motion pulling his paisley shirt tight against his broad chest. My eyes track the movement, lazily tracing every muscle outline peeping through the deep red material.

"There's no need to thank me. I owed you, remember?"

The cheerful glint in Cody's brown eyes is making me forget a lot of things at the moment. Things like why it would be a bad idea to invite the varsity captain back to my dorm.

One night of fun wouldn't hurt, would it?

"I don't know why you used the past tense. Last time I checked, you are only off the hook if I approved of your performance." I pretend to shoot him with my finger while Cody rolls his eyes.

"You O'Brien's are always changing the rules, aren't you?" He pushes off the wall and takes a step closer. One more step and our bodies would be pressed together.

"Somebody's got to keep you on your toes." I tilt my head back to look up at him, his shoulders almost completely blocking my view of the overhead lamp barely staying alive.

I've never been much of a climber, but I'd be willing to give those shoulders a go.

We stand like that, staring at each other for what seems like forever. Finally, I realize I'm still wearing the man's jacket and shrug it off.

That's probably what he's been waiting for.

"Why'd you do it?" The question leaves my lips as I pass the jacket back to him.

"Do what?"

"You know," I wave my hands in the air like I just discovered mime was my sole reason for living, "For pretending we were together back there."

I was surprised when Cody started the charade, but mostly relieved. Having to admit one's single status, or worse, a just-friends situation is so much worse after witnessing a cute couple fake fight over the retelling of their love story.

"Oh, yeah. No worries." Cody shrugs as if he didn't just save me from a long night of single itis. All the single ladies out there know what I'm talking about.

"Why'd you do it?" I repeat my question, watching closely for a reaction. Cody falls silent, his jaw clenching slightly as if the interrogation is starting to make him uncomfortable.

Interesting.

"You know, Mo always goes on about how much of a stand-up, honest guy you are. But pretending to be my boyfriend back there doesn't fit with the wholesome vibe you've got going on. So, why did you do it? Why did you play pretend?"

Cody's eyes darken and a line furrows between his brows. But still, he remains silent.

Damn the stubborn man and his powers of resistance.

Tapping my fingers against my lips, I look at him in mock contemplation, "Something doesn't add up here, Ellsworth. Mind helping a girl out?"

He gives a slight shake of the head, so subtle I almost miss it. The muscles popping along his jawline are hard to miss, though.

Not that I'm going to complain about the view, but the man is going to need dentures by the time he's thirty if he keeps that up.

I take half a step closer, bringing me well within touching distance.

My heart starts to pound at the close proximity, my breaths becoming more and more shallow. Cody, for his part, doesn't seem to be breathing at all, just waiting for my next move.

"I think maybe you like breaking character, Ellsworth. I think maybe you like breaking the rules sometimes, being the rebel nobody expects the hardworking varsity captain to be."

My words are no louder than a whisper, but they manage to waken the energy between us. Our eyes have yet to break contact and suddenly the temptation to touch him feels too strong to resist.

So, I don't.

Cody exhales heavily as I press my hands against his chest. My eyes never leave his as I gently slide my hands up the front of his shirt, up and around the back of his neck.

"I think you're wrong." Cody's voice comes out raspy, the growl-like sound sending a shiver down my spine.

"Well, I guess there's only one way to find out."

Pulling him down to my level, I don't give him a chance to think before I press my lips against his.

Cody

Stella O'Brien is kissing me.

I am kissing Stella O'Brien.

Different variations of that same thought run through my head like a victory lap stuck on repeat. I would be lying if I said I hadn't thought about kissing Stella before now.

Ever since that fateful morning at the gym, this girl has plagued my mind from the moment I wake up to my last thought before I fall asleep.

And now it's finally happening.

Stella's small hands impatiently tug at my neck, bringing me closer to her mouth that has yet to come up for air. Our tongues tangle together like the desperately needed oxygen will be found if we just keep searching. She nips my bottom lip and I groan, the unforgotten semi in my jeans springing to life once more.

Stella finally breaks contact for air, and I drop down to her neck, leaving a trail of gentle kisses along the narrow slope and down to the top of her collarbone. My hands trail down the curve of her ass and grip the top of her thighs, lifting her up to my height and spinning us around to use the wall for leverage.

Grabbing my face, Stella brings my mouth back to hers, kissing me through a moan as she grinds against the bulge in my jeans. I kiss her back hungrily, using my body as a cage to keep her where I want her.

I couldn't tell you how long we stayed like that: lips locked, Stella's legs around my waist, callused hands trying unsuccessfully to rip through western wear. All I know is one minute my senses are being overridden by a savage pixie and the next someone is awkwardly clearing their throat behind us.

"Oh hey, Stella. I thought that was you." My lust-filled brain clears just enough for me to realize we are still standing in front of the entrance to Stella's residence building.

Where anyone and everyone can see us.

Oops.

I gently lower Stella back to the ground, holding onto her arm as she steadies herself. After she gives me a dazed nod, I gently release her and turn to see none other than my favourite rookie and his girlfriend standing by the residence door.

"Hey Lou! Yup, it's me."

Stella nervously tucks a strand of hair behind her ear and I have to bite back a smile at the chaotic state of her hair. Her cowgirl hat got knocked off in our make out session and my hands made quick work of messing up Stella's normally impeccable mane.

I make eye contact with Wes' girlfriend, who immediately blushes deep red like she was the one caught doing something naughty. Wes, on the other hand, seems to be speechless for the first time in his life.

"Good to see you, Wes." I give him a nod but he just gapes in return.

"You just... her... what?"

Swivelling his head between the two of us, Wes looks more dazed than Stella did when I put her back on the ground.

"He was just making sure I got home safely. Right, Ellsworth?" Stella's lip gloss is all but gone, her toothy smile shining through every feature on her face.

"You got it, O'Brien." I smile back at her when the bomb hits.

I kissed Maurice O'Brien's younger sister.

Guilt floods my system, the damaging evidence blazingly obvious. I should have walked her home and left like an actual gentleman. Mo made me responsible for her protection and wellbeing, and yet her hair looks like someone manhandled her against a wall.

Oh God. I manhandled Mo's baby sister against a wall.

And she really enjoyed it. So did you.

I push the devil voice aside and try my best to tune in to the conversation going on around me.

"... were going to grab some pizza and watch a movie if you'd like to join?"

All three of them are looking at me expectedly and it takes a few seconds for me to connect the dots.

Mo is going to kill me.

Panicked, I blurt out the first thing that comes to mind, "I, uh, actually have to get going. Early morning practice and all that."

Wes shoots me a look at the blatant lie, but I am already heading for the door.

"I'll catch you later, okay?" I steal one last glance at Stella who looks back with disappointment etched across her face.

All three of them stay silent as I push open the door and step into the bitter cold, the residence door swinging shut behind me. Ignoring the tug in my chest, I start trudging back to my car, wishing with each step that doing the right thing didn't feel so wrong.

Chapter 9

Cody

He knows.

Maurice O'Brien knows I kissed his younger sister. That is the only reason I can think of why he's calling me this early in the morning.

I stare at the name flashing across my phone and take a deep breath.

I knew I would have to own up to it at some point, I'm not the type of guy who sweeps things under the rug, but I thought I would have more than six hours to prepare myself. And, you know, clear the air with Stella before getting the shit kicked out of me by her older brother.

Fuck.

Squeezing my eyes closed, I press accept.

"Ellsworth! About damn time, since when does it take four rings for you to answer?" Mo's booming voice fills my room, doing nothing to help the guilt clenching in my stomach.

Well, since I shoved my tongue down your sister's throat last night and ravished her against a wall, I was a little nervous to take your call.

I wince against the thought, "Sorry man, I just woke up."

"Well, well, well. Look who has finally learned how to sleep in."

I can't tell if Mo's cheerfulness is just a strategy to draw me in and get me to drop my guard or if it's genuine. My nerves are shot and now I'm questioning everything.

This is why you don't break the bro code.

"What can I do for you?" Defensiveness creeps into my tone but there's nothing I can do to stop it.

"I just wanted to check in on my favourite rookie. Am I still allowed to do that?"

Despite the circumstances, I find myself smiling, "You aren't supposed to have favourites, Mo. Favourites lead to biases."

"Please, it's only human nature to have a favourite, that's what makes for healthy competition. If no one is vying for your spot, then it's not a spot worth fighting for."

I shake my head with a sigh. If anybody can throw out bold statements with the confidence of a balding fifty-year-old man, it's Mo.

"Anyways, that's not what I called you about." His voice cracks through my phone and my shoulders tense, waiting for the inevitable.

Ass whooping, here I come.

"What are your plans for the break? Are you heading home to see Janet?"

I blink rapidly, struggling to comprehend why the questions sound like actual questions and not an angry accusation.

"Uh, yeah I'm heading home but my mom's gone on vacation with her new boyfriend." I slump against my headboard, doing my best not to feel relieved at the turn in conversation.

I should still feel guilty, I should.

But it's hard when a part of me is still celebrating the fact Stella's lips were firmly pressed against mine a few hours ago.

Idiot.

"Janet's found herself a new beau? Good for her. He must have passed the test if you're letting them vacation together."

I sigh, pushing last night's activities to the back of my mind, "Hank is one of the good ones. He treats her like a princess and that's all I can ask for."

I turn my head to glance at the photo frame gracing my nightstand. Taken a week before my first day of university, my mother and I had gotten one of my new neighbours to take it, both of us standing in front of the house I'm still living in. My mom was already proudly wearing a Proud Taber Mom t-shirt, even though I hadn't attended any classes yet. Her arm is thrown around my shoulders with clear elation while I stand next to her with an equally wide grin breaking my face.

After all those summers of mowing lawns and bussing tables, I had finally made enough money to attend university. And my mom had been my support system every step of the way.

"Pleased to hear it. I actually called to invite you to come down for a few days over the break, but if your mom's away, why don't you come stay with us the whole time? That way you won't be alone for Christmas."

I freeze, unable to decide if my heart is pounding with excitement or terror at the thought of spending more alone time with Stella.

And her older brother.

"I couldn't intrude on you guys like that. The break is to spend time with family."

A heavy sigh comes down the line, "Don't make me get all gushy, Ellsworth. You know I'll do it."

I push myself off my bed and start pacing the floor, "Thank you for the offer, Mo. I really appreciate it but I just... can't."

"That's it. I'm going to do it. I'm breaking out my gushy side."

I hear an exaggerated exhale on the other end of the line, not unlike what you'd hear from an Olympic swimmer as he mounts the blocks.

The dramatics run thick throughout the entire O'Brien family.

"I think of you like a brother, Ellsworth. And that makes you family." Taking a moment to clear his throat, Mo continues, "And family doesn't abandon family. So, I will pick your ass up Tuesday after morning practice and you can stay at my place as long as you want. Got it?"

I shake my head, "Shouldn't Stella get a say in this? It's her break too."

"She'll be ecstatic, she loves hanging out with you. Plus, you're one of the few people who doesn't get scared by her temper. You would be doing *me* a favour by tagging along."

I grimace, thinking of Stella's crestfallen face when I ran away last night. I owe her a huge apology along with an explanation for my actions.

"I don't know, man..."

"Ellsworth. This is not up for discussion. I will pick you up Tuesday, 8:30AM sharp. Have a bag packed and ready to go." He hangs up the phone, ending the call.

Shit.

Stella

CODY: *We need to talk.*

I toss my phone across Lou's bed where I have been lounging all morning. Her comforter is nowhere near as soft or as fuzzy as mine, but being in her presence more than makes up for it.

"Isn't it a good thing he wants to talk? Like wouldn't it be worst if he was pretending the whole thing didn't happen?" Lou twirls a wavy strand around her finger, eyes scrunched up in thought.

"That's exactly the problem, hon."

I heave myself onto my stomach for a change of scenery. Instead of staring at a moldy ceiling, now I'm admiring sticky laminate.

It's good to broaden one's horizons.

"Cody wants to talk because he regrets kissing me." Ouch. Saying the words out loud hurt a lot more than just thinking them.

Lou tilts her head, her sitting position at her dorm desk separating us by a whole two feet.

"Didn't you kiss him?"

I lift my head high enough to give her a glare, "Not the point, Lou."

"Right, sorry." She blushes faintly, the only telltale her social anxiety continues to linger even after all we've been through together. It breaks my heart to still see it, but I am proud to have watched her grow these last few months.

"No need to be sorry, I'm just in a mood." I huff, dropping my gaze back down to the horrid colour choice.

Why would anyone think speckled brown is a good colour?

"What I'm trying to say is, Cody wants to pull the whole *that was a mistake, let's promise to just forget the whole thing* charade with me." I frown at a drifting clump of hair, not sure whether the sick feeling is from my close proximity or the thought of Cody regretting last night.

"Do *you* regret kissing Cody?"

I hum to myself, taking a moment to think about my answer.

Do I regret kissing Cody? At the time, absolutely not. But the way he ran away the moment our friends showed up left a sour taste in my mouth. Not that his subpar reaction did anything to lessen my sexual frustration last night.

Curse those broad shoulders.

And that jawline.

And those eyes.

And those... ENOUGH.

I sigh, torn between wanting to punch myself and wanting to punch the varsity captain who haunted me all night long.

"Honestly? I don't regret kissing Cody. A part of me wishes I do, just so this next part will be easier, but I don't."

Lou nods, "That makes sense. Although he could be wanting to talk to see if you'd want to go out with him. You never know."

Pushing myself up on my elbows, I slide further down the bed, putting some space between my face and the clump of hair.

"I highly doubt it. That would be going against his precious mentor, and that's not something Ellsworth has ever been able to do."

"Would Mo really be that mad if you two dated?"

I pause, "I've never actually thought about Mo's reaction before. He would definitely be upset if we snuck around behind his back, but I'm not sure what he would do if we were upfront about it."

Shooting a look at my roommate, I don't give my heart a second drop of hope, "But that isn't an option at this point, so there's no point in considering it."

"Right. So, what's your plan than?" Lou picks a piece of lint off her Green Day t-shirt and flicks it onto the ground. I try not to flinch when I see it land near the unspeakable clump.

"Mo is coming to pick me up Tuesday, so I could take the coward's way out..." Lou's eyes widen at my confession, one I would never act on but will dream about it until this painful encounter is over.

Not that I can complain. I was, after all, the one who kissed him.

"...*but* I don't have it in me to avoid confrontation. I'm just going to get it over with, so it doesn't fester into something worse."

O'Brien's don't run away from their problems. We face them head on. Remember that, Stella.

"Guess you'll be needing this." Lou shuffles over and picks up my phone, taking a second to wipe God-knows what off the screen before handing it over.

"I guess so." I grumble under my breath as I re-open the damning message.

CODY: We need to talk.

The message stares back at me as my mind goes blank.

The only thing I can think about right now is how much I don't want to do this and how badly Lou needs to vacuum her floor.

"Shit." I tap aggressively, hit send, then throw my phone back on the bed.

"Good job!" Lou leans over for a high five just as my phone beeps with an incoming text. We both scream, undoubtedly for very different reasons.

Lou gasps, one hand clutching her chest in fright, "That was the worst post-text celebration ever. Hashtag unsend."

I groan, reaching back down to go through the motions all over again.

CODY: We need to talk.
ME: So, talk.

Not going to lie, that last text may have come off as a little aggressive. Probably should have added an emoji to soften the blow.

CODY: In person. Are you free tonight?

ME: I have a late workout planned. Does 7PM work?

CODY: Yup. I'll meet you at the gym.

"So? What did he say?" Lou looks at me hopefully and I don't have it in me to extinguish the light in her eyes.

"We're going to talk after my gym session tonight." I do my best to keep my voice upbeat, but it sounds fake even to my ears.

Lou gives me an encouraging thumbs up, "I will be here with a tub of ice cream and a really bad movie so you have something to look forward to."

I give her a hug as the unspoken message hangs between us.

She'll be waiting in case I need to be put back together again.

Chapter 10

♥

Cody

"What the actual hell, Cody?"

We don't make it ten feet from the gym entrance before Stella explodes. She whirls around to face me, index finger jabbing my chest hard enough to leave a bruise.

"You made me look like an idiot yesterday. You better start talking. Now."

I sigh, gently taking her hand and tugging her into an empty corridor. There isn't a lot of students wandering the halls at this time of evening, but this discussion calls for some privacy.

"I'm sorry Stel."

The words I need to say and the words I want to say stumble over themselves in the race to the surface, turning my cohesive sentence into an intangible mess so I'm left with no words at all.

"Is that it? Pretty sure you could have messaged me that."

Stella rips her hand from mine and takes a step back to increase the distance between us. Every cell in my body wants to counteract the action and close the gap, but the look she's giving me right now makes the Ice Age seem like a balmy vacation.

"Look, I really don't want to be near you right now. Say what you need to say then leave." Stella spits out the words, her topknot slowly unraveling as though it too can't stand the sight of me.

"When it comes to leaving, we both know you've got that move down."

Ouch.

But not uncalled for.

"I shouldn't have left the way I did." My voice comes out gruff as I push past the lump in my throat. It feels like a small victory until I see Stella's defensive position hasn't budged an inch.

"No kidding."

I didn't think the hostility could grow any stronger, but she keeps proving me wrong.

"I've wanted to kiss you for a long time, Stel."

Stella's jaw drops, her eyes widening as my admission sinks in.

I shrug, condemning myself to the honest route, "It's true. Ever since that first day I met you, I've wanted to get to know you better."

My eyes flick to her lips, "I've wanted to know what you taste like."

Stella's mouth snaps shut, a red flush spreading across her neck as her eyes take on a shine that has nothing to do with post-workout endorphins.

Great. Now we're both turned on.

So much for having a game plan.

"But you're my mentor's younger sister. *Mighty Mo's* younger sister." I swallow thickly, pushing past the urge to abort mission. "We can't ever be together, Stella. If I were to hurt you, Mo would never forgive me. *I* would never forgive me."

A single tear hits her cheek and I hastily wipe it away before it can leave a permanent mark on my heart.

Meeting with Stella tonight, I was expecting anger. Part little man syndrome, part younger sibling syndrome, Stella is a hothead through and through but once she lets off some steam, she's normally pretty quick to calm down.

What I wasn't expecting was the vulnerability shining through every pore of her being.

"What if you didn't hurt me?" Her question is barely above a whisper, as if all the wind has disappeared from her sails of fury and taken her voice with it.

Chest aching with a pain I've never felt before, I open up my arms and she steps into the embrace. I pull her close, blinking against the burning sensation building in my own eyes.

"I'm sorry, Stel. That's not a risk I'm willing to make."

We stand like that, protecting each other from the outside world for seconds or minutes, I couldn't tell you.

What I can tell you is it felt like the beginning of the end of something that never truly started.

Eventually, Stella pulls far enough away to rest her chin on my chest. Her tilted face and our close proximity makes it easy to read her expression, but instead of seeing bitter sorrow reflected back at me, I'm met with a calm stare.

A calm stare that makes me think the undertow is about to pull me under.

"So, here's the thing."

Here we go.

"When you say you aren't *willing* you mean you are choosing not to fight for us, right?"

"Did you not listen to a thing I just said?"

"No, I did." She ducks out from my embrace, pacing through her argument two feet in front of me.

I try not to notice the way her black leggings cling to her backside, but the thin material leaves little room for the imagination.

"But you basically admitted to taking the easy way out."

Is she joking?

"Did you miss the part where I said *I want to kiss you*?" My voice is slowly getting louder, drawing looks from the only person to walk down this corridor in the last ten minutes.

Naturally.

"Mm, I did like that part." She licks her lips and smiles at me in a way that has me looking at those leggings again, except this time I'm picturing them on my bedroom floor.

Focus, Ellsworth. This is what got you in trouble in the first place.

"BUT that doesn't change the fact that you're taking the coward's way out."

I cross my arms, our defensive positions reversed from minutes earlier, "How do you figure?"

"Well…" Stella holds up three fingers and starts ticking them off, "First, you are too much of a coward to simply *ask* my brother if he would be okay with us dating. Second, if you didn't want to involve the great Mighty Mo, you could have grown a backbone and fought against any objections he might have."

She rolls her eyes at the mention of her brother's title but still manages to check off her final finger with a flourish, "And last but not least, you didn't even ask how I felt or took into consideration what I want."

Leave it to me to find the only girl who aggravates me as much as she amazes me.

I think I hate her.

Stella

If I took a shot every time Cody clenched his jaw, I would be comatose by now.

Watching him get more and more riled up every time I say the word "coward" has quickly become my new favourite past time.

Sadistic? Maybe.

Truthful? Absolutely.

I'm embarrassed to admit Cody's little monologue got me to the point of tears – more like tear, singular – but witnessing the honesty being ripped from his body did something to me. It broke a damn inside that I didn't know existed until a tear slid out from the hard shell I created when I found out my mother was never coming home.

I'll be the first to admit, I cry over a lot of things, but boys? Relationships? Discussing and ending the theoretical idea of an us?

Let me put it to you this way: there wasn't a single tear shed when my first serious boyfriend dumped me weeks after the accident.

I don't cry over failed relationships. Never have and thought I never would.

And then I had to go and meet Cody freaking Ellsworth.

I think I hate him.

"You…" Cody trails off, annoyance seeping through his tone while his gaze searches my face for the answer he's looking for.

"Yes, Cody?" I beam back at him, adding another shot to the count.

I'll have to tell Wes about this drinking game. Someone ought to enjoy my ingenious brand of revenge.

He sighs, looking up at the ceiling for the answers my face didn't offer him.

"You always take the hard road, don't you?"

"If you don't challenge yourself, you don't change yourself." I quote the words without thinking, the O'Brien mantras rolling through my mind like a jukebox spitting out its favourite tunes.

Come on Stella, how can you expect to grow if you're never put in uncomfortable situations? Do the circuit. Again.

Are you really going to settle for average? O'Brien's aren't average, Stella. We succeed. We set the example. It's about time you played your part.

My father's voice rings through my ears, the echoing tone sharpened with each passing month his beloved wife lay buried underground.

"That's not the point, Stel."

I blink back to present and find a frowning varsity captain looking in my direction. Guess it wasn't the right time to break out the motivational pep talks.

"Then what is the point, Cody? What is your point?"

I feel like kicking a chair at his pigheadedness but there's no chair in sight. I contemplate using his shin as a substitute but that probably wouldn't help my cause.

"My point is I'm not in a position right now to pursue a relationship with you." He presses his fingers against his nose as if a headache's coming on, "And I don't know if there ever will be a right time."

"Right time? Oh, Cody." I throw my head back and laugh until I'm wheezing. "Didn't getting your head bashed in last semester teach you anything?"

He shoots me a look at the head bashing comment, but I continue, "There is no such thing as the right time. We're always going to be too busy or too complicated for it to work. You can't look at it from a rational point of view, Ellsworth. You've got to let it happen and see where it takes you."

Cody shakes his head, choosing not to listen to a single thing I said, "Please don't put me in this position, Stel. Where I have to choose between you or Mo."

I can see in his eyes that his mind's already made up.

Stupid boy.

"Fine, have it your way. But when you finally pull your head out of your ass, you'll realize what a huge mistake you made."

I look him dead in the eye, refusing to be the one to break contact, "And when that happens, I hope you remember one thing. I won't be waiting."

Chapter 11

Stella

"What am I going to do without you?" Lou sighs, tugging the ends of her baggy t-shirt past anything considered to be fashionable or flattering.

"Oh, Lou. It's just three weeks, we will be back in this cramped living space before you know it." I'm throwing the last of my clothes into the open suitcase lying on the ground, my other two already zipped up and ready to go by the door.

Hey, it's still three weeks. A girl needs to have options when it comes to attire.

"I know but I'm going to miss you." Lou sniffs slightly, her downcast eyes looking at my dorm's slightly-cleaner-but-still-unfortunate floor.

"I'm going to miss you too, hon. Come here." I walk over and wrap my arms tightly around my best friend, "I'll Facetime you every day, okay? Plus, I can't wait to hear how meeting the parents go."

Lou squeezes me back with a groan, "I can't believe Wes talked me into spending a whole week at his house."

I pat her back in reassurance, "The good news is he gets to suffer the same treatment for the last week of break."

"That is true." Lou's face brightens, "And my dad is supposed to be home for a couple of days this time, so he'll get to meet Wes too."

Poor guy. From what I've heard of Lou's ecologist father, the man spends most his time talking about work even on the rare occasion he isn't at work. Hope Wes has brushed up on Canadian ecological systems.

"This will be a good test for you two. If you don't hate each other after spending a whole week with each other's family, you two can get through anything."

Lou sighs, "I hope so. Do you need help with that?"

The question catches me mid-grunt, while I'm trying to use my body weight to get the zipper of my suitcase to close. This is probably why most people don't bring all their clothes home over break, but I've already committed.

The O'Brien's are stubborn, remember?

"Could you just..." I gesture wildly to the other side of the suitcase and by some miracle Lou gets my message. She walks over and climbs aboard, the two of us barely managing to stay on top of a wobbling suitcase.

"I've almost got it!" I tug painfully at the small zipper, the piece of metal cutting into my fingers as I heave it forward, barely moving it an inch.

"Don't think I want to know what's going on right now."

The sound of a male's voice fills the room and Lou immediately stops squirming beside me. She snaps upright in a way that tells me exactly who has found his way to our dorm.

I huff, not bothering to look at my brother as the zipper teasingly shifts forward, "Feel free to take the other suitcases to the car. I'll be out in a sec."

Mo chuckles, the familiar sound making me smile, "And miss the show? Hell, no. Nice to see you again, Lou."

I'm almost completely upside down at this point but I still manage to see my roommate blush at the friendly nod my brother gives her.

Even with Wes on the scene, I can't blame the girl. My older brother has a certain aura that commands attention. And when he chooses to bestow that attention on to you, you feel like the most special person on this planet. Doesn't help that he looks like a character from a gladiator movie.

You know the movie where shirtless guys fight to death? Gerard Butler in all his glory? Yeah, Mo didn't get his nickname Mighty just for his moves on the lacrosse field.

"Nice to see you too, Mo." Lou squeaks out the words, her fingers nervously fiddling with the daisy charm on her necklace.

Thank God blood relation and sibling bickering made me immune to his charms.

"Done!"

After forever and a day, the zipper finally gives way and my third suitcase zips itself closed. I hop off the pink material without an ounce of elegance or grace and go charging towards my brother.

"Hey, stranger." He chuckles as I tackle him in a hug.

"Hey, yourself. You ready to go?" His pale blue eyes do a sweep of my room, a smirk tugging at his mouth when his eyes flick past my closet that is almost completely empty.

"Give me a few minutes to say goodbye and then I'll be ready to go."

He nods, shooting Lou a smile before ducking out of the room. I turn back towards my roommate, the girl who has slowly become a permanent fixture in my life and in my heart.

My bravado from earlier starts to wear off and I feel my lips tremble as I hug her one last time, "We'll talk every day, okay?"

Lou isn't that tall, but I still have to go on my tiptoes to whisper in her ear. Short people really aren't built for sentimental moments.

"Okay." Her voice trembles like she's also struggling to keep the emotions at bay.

"Oh! I almost forgot." I scurry over to my nightstand and pull out an artfully wrapped box that I spent way too long perfecting weeks ago.

"Merry Christmas, Sis." I go to pass her the gift, but Lou bolts from the room, leaving me standing there awkwardly with the gift dangling from my fingertips.

At least the wrapping looks amazing.

Lou reappears two minutes later, huffing from her 10-meter sprint. She's also clutching something in her hands, making my heart pound with excitement. I can't remember the last time someone who wasn't my brother bought me something.

"Merry Christmas, Stella. Thank you for always being there for me." She's still panting from the short burst of cardio, and I almost laugh when we make the trade.

If I live for cardio circuits, Lou lives to avoid them.

Lou gingerly pokes the pristine white bow decorating her box, a crease appearing between her brows, "It looks too pretty to open."

I shake my head with a smile, "Go on, I've been waiting for you to tear that apart."

Okay, that may have been a lie.

But *I am* excited to see her reaction for what lies inside.

Carefully pulling at the bow, Lou slowly peels back the paper and gasps when she lifts the lid, "Oh, Stella. It's lovely."

She holds up a silver bracelet with a single guitar-shaped charm hanging off the end. Her boyfriend stole my mojo with the cutesy initial and flower necklace, so I had to go for her other passion: alternative rock music.

"Now you'll always have something to remember our Punk Rockers Event by."

Lou beams as she slides the delicate chain around her wrist, "I love it. This is so much better than those leather pantsuits. Thank you, Stella."

She shoots a quick look at the gift still untouched in my hands and blushes deeply, "I'm sorry about the wrapping paper. It was a bit of a last-minute situation."

I laugh, waving away her concerns, "The obituary section from last week's newspaper is all I've ever wanted for Christmas."

Lou gasps, "It's not the obituary section, is it? Oh, Stella, I'm so sorry. I thought I used the weather segment."

The seriousness in her expression only makes me laugh harder.

"Cheers to making it another year!" My hilarity is contagious and soon we are both cracking up, tears running down our faces as I gasp for air.

"I'm just joking, Lou. You didn't have to get me anything. This means... This means a lot."

Still giggling uncontrollably, Lou gestures towards the gift, "Don't thank me yet. It could be last year's obituary hidden in there."

I grin, tearing into the clumsily wrapped gift. A simple black frame tumbles into my hands, a roommate selfie Lou and I took during one of our many outings this semester. We are smiling cheek-to-cheek, friendship and happiness overflowing from the captured moment.

My breath catches as I read the sparkly sticker letters added to the bottom of the frame.

Roommates for now, Sisters for life.

"I, uh, noticed you didn't have any pictures in your room, so I though this could be the first." Lou nervously tucks a strand of hair behind her ear, my silence doing nothing to help her discomfort.

Truth is, I'm speechless.

"No, it's just..." I trail off, unsure how to explain the love and gratitude flowing through my veins. "It's just so thoughtful. Thank you, Lou." Emotions clog my throat as I pull her back for yet another hug.

"I know exactly where to put it."

Cody

"But like, what if her parents don't like me?"

Wes pales, his characteristic confidence nowhere in sight, "Oh God. What if her *dad* doesn't like me?"

I hold back a laugh, clapping the rookie on the back.

"You're overthinking this, man. Just be yourself." I pause before adding, "But maybe don't flirt with the mom this time."

Wes groans, "I can't help it. That woman is like fine wine."

Walking by with a dissembled lacrosse net thrown over his shoulder, Nico snorts, "Please. You're so whipped at this point the MILF won't get a second thought."

Hunter quips up from his position on the ground, "Wes finally found a girl to carry his balls around."

"I'll have you know," Using one hand to grab his junk, Wes uses the other to flip Hunter the bird. "My balls are exactly where Trip likes them."

"I can attest to that fact." Nico holds up his hand and earns himself a high five from his best friend, the junk holder.

I call for attention with a clap of my hands, "That was a good last practice, team. I've got to run but I hope everyone has a good break. Make decently smart decisions!"

"Who said anything about being decent?"

Nico's voice fades as I exit the gym, taking a quick detour to the locker room to grab my bag and change into some weather-appropriate clothes.

Now all that's left to do is appease a furious 4'11 platinum blonde for a 13-hour car drive.

∞

"What the hell is he doing here?" Stella's long braid whips back and forth as her head swivels between her brother and me.

It's safe to say I forgot to tell her about my new plans for the break.

"Ellsworth is joining us this year!" Mo cheerily shouts the words from inside the popped trunk, his wide frame all but disappearing into the back of the Cadillac with a large, bright pink suitcase.

"And you didn't think to clear that with me?" Stella's eyes flash angrily, her temper visibly rising behind the not-so-cool façade.

"Since when do you care if I bring friends home?"

Stella huffs, "When it happens to coincide with *my* break and the time *I* get to spend with my brother, I think I'm allowed to have an opinion on the topic."

Mo emerges from the trunk, his pressed pants and dress shirt completely crease-free from the action. His perfectly styled, light brown hair looks equally untouched.

Sometimes I wonder if he's photoshopped.

"I thought you and Ellsworth were tight. You talk about him all the time." Mo gestures towards my small duffel bag, "You want that in the back?"

"Nah, I'm good."

Sneaking a glance at Stella, I bite my cheek to keep from laughing at her pinkening face. At this point, I can't tell if it's from anger, embarrassment, or simply being in my presence.

"I don't talk about him all the time." She growls the words, climbs into the passenger seat, and slams the door shut.

Mo smirks, "She'll get over it. You talk about her just as much."

And there goes the smile from my face.

"Looks like you've got the back. It's good to see you, man." A charming smile and a hard back slap are all I get before Mo climbs into the driver's seat and starts the engine.

Here goes nothing.

Taking one last breath of sanity, I open the door and clamber in behind Stella.

The second my seatbelt clicks into place, her seat cranks back as far as possible, almost disabling me in the process. Within seconds, my leg space goes from comfortable to nonexistent, forcing me to shift sideways so I don't spend the entire drive kneeing Stella in the spine.

As tempting as that may be.

A young Justin Bieber starts crooning out of the speakers, the repetitive tune of my childhood only slightly less painful than my leg situation. An evil grin flashes at me through the side mirror and I sigh, leaning my head back and closing my eyes with defeat.

This is going to be a long drive.

Chapter 12

Stella

"Isn't BC the other way?"

Cody's genuine confusion is the only reason I chose the civil route and resist rolling my eyes. Instead, I let Mo take this one and continue relishing in the fact Cody's legs are significantly more cramped than they were half an hour ago.

I do love petty revenge.

"Sure is!" Mo shoots me a wink, providing absolutely no explanation for why we're heading towards Lethbridge instead of Crownest Pass.

I smirk, glancing out my window at the snow-covered corn fields lining either side of Mo's tinted windows. The clouds are hanging low today, making it difficult to see the white-peaked mountains standing guard in the distance.

If I'm being honest, besides those white-peaked beauties, the flat spans of prairie don't leave a lot to admire.

"Right, okay." Cody falls silent once more, letting my spectacular 2000s playlist fill the void in the car. We cruise for about twenty more minutes before slowing down to pass through another small town.

My humming pauses as I take in the rickety houses and faded business buildings lining the main road.

"Hey, isn't this where that club is..." I trail off, squinting at the passing signs in hope something will spark my memory.

"You're thinking of *Lifestyle*. That's in the next town over." Mo adjusts his grip on the steering wheel, his gaze focused on the road ahead.

Cody laughs from the backseat, "Oh yeah, I've heard of that one. Wes and Nico always have a good time there." He chuckles some more, "Last I heard, it's the rowdiest gay club in Southern Alberta. And if that's coming from those two, it must be true."

Through the side mirror, I watch Cody shake his head and smile. He mustn't have shaved this morning because stubble is starting to grow in, the dark blonde hair pulling unnecessary attention to that jawline.

Unnecessary because it draws enough attention on its own.

Cody catches me staring and I quickly avert my gaze to the frost-bitten tumbleweed blowing down the sidewalk. After a few minutes of sightseeing, I risk another glance only to find him staring right back at me. I freeze as our eyes lock, the reflection tethering us together while keeping us a safe distance apart.

Sums up our non-existent relationship well.

He leans forward, disappearing from my vantage point, and suddenly I feel warm air brush against the side of my neck. The whisper of contact triggers goosebumps to rise along my skin despite the heat Mo is blasting through the vents.

I feel Cody shift closer, his legs pressing hard into the back of my seat and into the base of my spine.

"Would you mind skipping this song? I'm not a fan."

His mouth is right next to my ear, the vibrations of his voice flowing through my body and mingling with my other senses. One inch to the left and my cheek would be pressed against his and I'd finally see what that scruff feels like.

Shame he had to ruin the moment with last night's conversation.

Ignoring the close proximity, I calmly reach for the audio controls, bypassing the skip option and making a beeline for the volume.

And I proceed to crank it.

Miley Cyrus' *Party in the USA* blasts through the speakers and I take it as my cue to start singing at the top of my lungs.

Off-key, of course.

My older brother, God bless him, either didn't hear Cody's comment or chose to take my side, because he turns the dial even higher and pretty soon, we are rocking a duet down the snow-covered roads.

Cody grunts and folds himself back into his seat, choosing to accept defeat in sullen silence.

The last bar of the song rings out, but Mo and I don't take a breath before launching into the next party anthem streaming from my phone. We keep the sibling car karaoke going all the way to Lethbridge, finally calling it quits when we arrive at our intermediate destination.

"Man, I've missed this." Mo gives me a smile that says more than I can explain, "It's good to have you back, Stel."

"It's good to be back." We grin at each other, but the bonding moment is cut short when a throat clears behind me.

"Did I miss something? Why are we at the Lethbridge airport?"

Mo turns to face our backseat passenger, "You didn't miss anything, we're just cutting our drive short. Stella isn't one for road trips."

I shudder in agreement. Motion medicine works to keep my nausea down, but it knocks me out harder than a horse tranquilizer.

Popping the trunk, Mo grabs two of my suitcases and I climb out to grab the last one, shooting Cody a glare when he tries to grab it for me. We head towards the check-in desk, bypassing the small terminals until we arrive at the private sector.

Mo pulls out his security clearance and a quick check of our IDs has the receptionist greeting us like long lost friends, "Mr. and Miss O'Brien, it is so nice to have you flying with us again."

"It's our pleasure, Stephanie."

Stephanie beams as if Mo's name tag reading was worthy of a Grammy. Cody snorts and I hold back a gag. I can't take this dog anywhere.

"If there's anything I can be of assistance with, please let me know." Giving Mo an obvious once-over, Stephanie hands each of us a clearance pass and waves us through.

I shoot my brother a look as we head to our designated hanger.

He smirks, "It's called exchanging pleasantries, Stella. You should look into it sometime."

"More like exchanging numbers. Tell me she slipped something with your clearance pass."

Mo doesn't even bother glancing at the piece of paper in his hand, "As if lovely Stephanie was going to be the one to break my streak. We're practically the same age."

I roll my eyes, "One octogenarian, Mo. One. That does not make you irresistible to women of all ages."

"Did or didn't I get that sweet little old timer's number?"

Cody's eyes go wide, "No way. You hit on a grandma?"

"Bethany was closer to my great grandma's age, but yes, we got along well."

Mo lifts his shoulder casually as if this was an everyday occurrence, "She was taking her first international cruise and wanted a way for me to keep in touch afterwards."

I laugh, "He got the number to some old folk's home down in New Jersey."

"Hey, Beth was thrilled to hear from me once they finally patched me through. Good thing she'd left me her room number as well."

I cackle at the memory, Cody's shock swiftly turning into suspicion.

"You're playing with me, aren't you?"

Mo grins, "If you don't believe me, just ask Stella."

Cody's eyes narrow as I wipe away tears, "Hey, don't look at me. I wasn't Bethany's shuffleboard partner for six weeks straight."

Cody opens his mouth to respond, but no words leave his lips as we step into the hanger.

Cody

Holy shit. I feel like Tom Cruise.

Small planes of every colour blind me as we enter the wing saved purposefully for people with enough money to avoid commercial flying altogether.

People like Mo and Stella, apparently.

"Do you always travel this way?" Awe seeps into my voice as I take in the shiny aircrafts, my aerospace and aviation knowledge desperately lacking as I gaze, dazed, upon all the different styles of entry-level jets.

"This is my first time flying out of Lethbridge, but yes, father is a majority shareholder in a couple of airline companies."

There's a slight grimace with Stella's response, as if discussing the degree of her family's wealth isn't something she's comfortable with.

"Oh."

A tow bar passes us by with a bright orange plane attached to the end. The spoiler hanging off the plane is easily the same size as my car.

Stella bites her lip, momentarily distracting me from the displays of wealth wheeling by.

"Did Mo never tell you?"

"Tell me what?"

"That we're..."

"Stella!" The man stationed in front of a beautiful blue and white stripped plane steps forward with a huge smile and a bushy grey moustache.

"Uncle Johnson!"

An equally bright smile takes over Stella's face as they meet in an embrace. "It's been way too long. How are the pups holding up?"

"Oh, the old girls are doing just fine. Still getting spoilt like there's no tomorrow."

"Aunt Jose?"

"Even more spoilt than the dogs."

Stella throws her head back and laughs, looking more carefree than I've ever seen her.

Johnson shakes his head, watching his niece with blatant adoration, "I've missed you, my dear. How is university treating you?"

"It's been a really great experience. My roommate is the loveliest girl, I think she might even be my soul sister."

Johnson chuckles, his crisp uniform crinkling as he bends down to collect Stella's suitcase.

"That is something your mother would say. I am so pleased to hear…"

"It's nice to watch, isn't it?" Mo's voice drags my attention from the family reunion. The look on his face is one I've never seen before. It's not jealous exactly, it's almost… wistful.

"You two aren't close?" I ask the question, watching for a reaction.

"Oh, we are but we got the chance to catch up on the way here."

Mo nods his head towards his sister who is still chatting away without a care in the world, "She's not like that with everyone. It takes a lot for her to open up."

I glance back at Stella, her long braid falling past mid-back as she happily helps Johnson store the luggage in the plane's undercarriage. Her puffy winter jacket hides any trace of the fitness model underneath but suddenly my mind is back at the gym when I accidentally spotted her tattoo.

A tattoo she never once mentioned.

I wouldn't flatter myself by saying Stella and I are close, but I've never considered Stella and me to be… well, not *not* close.

We're friends, definitely, but besides being regular gym buddies, how well do I really know her?

I shut my eyes and try to conjure the facts I *do* know about Stella.

She's close to her brother, that much is obvious, she loves dancing, attending terrible residence events, hanging out with her roommate, singing along to terrible music, bickering with me at the gym every morning… but those all feel surface level. Things that even Wes would know about her. Maybe even Nico.

They don't know what her lips taste like.

But even that doesn't feel like enough.

Watching Stella climb the stairs, her small frame bounding up them with an endless supply of energy, I'm hit with a sudden urge to fill the gaps. To find a way to bridge the distance Stella puts between herself and the outside world and finally see what lays inside.

"Welcome aboard Cirrus Vision SF50, Ellsworth. We call her CV for short." Throwing me a wink, my mentor turns and follows his sister up the stairs.

Shifting my duffel back to my other shoulder, I take one last glance at the shiny exterior of the aircraft.

Wish me luck, CV.

I have a feeling I'm going to need it.

Chapter 13

Stella

Home sweet home.

Well, more like back at the family house. It's hard to call a house a home when you've lost the one person who made it feel that way. To say the halls have hollowed since my mother's death would be a gross understatement. One even my father couldn't disagree with.

Our car slows to a crawl as we approach the gates of Shaughnessy Heights. You need a six-digit code to get into the community, never mind the voice recognition needed to access someone's driveway.

It's overkill to say the least.

Our driver punches in the code and the gates slowly open before us. Snow-covered hedges come into view, their artificial shape and strategic placement meant to maximize homeowner's security. And privacy.

Something I've learned over the years is rich people don't have neighbours, they just have homeowners in inconvenient locations.

My air pods drown out Cody and Mo's voices as I gaze out the passenger window, watching dusk descend upon the sky, making the hedge-shaped silhouettes stretch farther along the road in front of us.

Past the gates it's only a five-minute drive to our house and soon the familiar slope of our driveway comes into sight.

Pod lights flick on as the sky continues to darken, lighting up the winding stretch of road as we descend onto my father's property. The manicured lawns gracing each side of the driveway are covered in a few feet of snow and the frozen crystals sparkle at us as we drive past. Our driver pulls to a stop just beside the marble fountain now doubling as an ice sculpture, with the fortress that is my family home looming before us.

I pop out my earphones just as Cody mutters, "Holy shit."

Mo chuckles, "Wait till you see the inside."

I'll admit, I may have been a bit misleading with the "house" reference earlier, but it's weird to think of my family house as a mansion. Don't get me wrong, I understand that most people don't have an indoor pool, a steam room, and two different gyms in their household, but calling my house a mansion just feels pompous.

Plus, that would ruin the surprise.

Mo tips the driver and we all climb out of the car. Cody almost trips himself trying to crane his neck back far enough to take in the stone arches towering above him. The sunset responds to the moment perfectly, the bloodred sky bringing out the smooth white exterior of the sprawling mansion.

I barely get a chance to appreciate the view before a deep voice pulls my attention to the figure standing under the stone columns barricading the entrance.

"You're late."

Even from ten feet away, I can see displeasure seeping through my father's handsome face. He hasn't aged much since I last saw him, his skin remains mostly winkle-free, and the blue cashmere sweater and dress pants look impeccable. His formal attire is fitted to perfection, casually outlining the same dominating build Mo has.

That is to say, strong and built to perfection.

"Unexpected glacial winds blew in and added a few minutes to our flight time." Mo responds easily, as if my father's earlier comment was a question instead of a statement.

Cody walks forward with an outstretched hand, "Cody Ellsworth, sir. It's nice to finally meet you."

"Jonathan O'Brien."

Ignoring the handshake offer, Jonathan turns and blinks down at me, as if he forgot how to properly embrace his daughter after months of being apart.

"Stella."

"Father."

One more blink and that's it. That's all I get for a reunion.

"Have you eaten?" Jonathan directs the question at Mo, the undesignated leader of our group.

"Not yet."

"I'll get Margaret to prepare something for you."

Taking the suitcase from my hand, Jonathan nods at the boys, "Leave your bags here. Stewart will see to them."

He turns and leads the way into the foyer, the elegant chandelier hanging high and proud from the arched ceiling. Once upon a time, the chandelier cast a warm light on the massive room, but even the electric candles have grown colder since my mother's passing.

"So, you guys are rich?" Cody whispers the question to me, his gaze widening as he takes in the spiral staircase to our left.

"My father is a very wealthy man, yes. My own state of affairs, however, is a very different matter." I lean closer, enjoying the scent of Cody's Old Spice deodorant.

"Why didn't you tell me?" His eyes flick to mine, and I'm surprised to see a hint of disappointment buried in the molten brown.

"It's not the easiest thing to bring up in a conversation. Plus, we aren't that close."

My retort hits its mark and Cody pulls away, ending our conversation.

Jonathan marches us towards the dining room, floor-to-ceiling windows offering an unparalleled view of the Vancouver skyline. The city lights glow in the distance, the busy bustle of traffic one endless cycle.

It's beautiful in an isolating way.

Margaret must have been messaged on the walk over because three plates of steaming food are already set on the table by the time we arrive. We all take a seat, my father taking the head position, with Mo and Cody on his right and me on his left. He watches Cody carefully as the varsity captain takes his first few bites, waiting for a sign of weakness via poor table manners.

Surprising us all, Cody picks up the appropriate fork and begins respectably eating his food. I spy Jonathan give a small nod of approval before turning his attention to me.

"How did your first semester go, Stella?"

Most parents are looking for the generic response, one that gives them an overall summary of the experience, like how you are enjoying it and did you make any new friends. Unfortunately, my father is not like most parents.

"Four As and one B. Actively participated in five clubs, two of which held extracurricular events that were off campus. Gym progression has been steady."

Cody raises an eyebrow at the flat monotone I have spent the last two years perfecting.

Jonathan nods, "What class was it that dropped your academic standing?"

"International management."

I jab a big piece of vegetable pasta into my mouth as a stalling technique. My father would rather cut off his own arm than hear someone speak with their mouth full.

"That is disappointing, Stella. Very disappointing." He leans forward, his handsome features so much harsher than they used to be.

"What are you going to do to fix that?"

In my peripheral, I see Cody open his mouth to say something but Mo elbows him before he gets the chance. A silent conversation battles itself out across the table, the guest not yet understanding the patriarchy this household follows.

I swallow my food with a sigh, "I won't let it happen again, father. The professor marked subjectively through essays, and he did not like my writing."

"That sounds like an excuse. Do O'Brien's make excuses?"

"No, we make results. I won't let it happen again."

"Good." Pleased with my submission, Jonathan shifts the conversation to his eldest, "Have there been any advancements with MacNeil Incorporated?"

Mo takes his turn, answering the questions as straightforward as possible. Like the handshake Cody never received, small talk is pointless with my father. His only interests lie with an individual's achievements and personal growth, two personality traits he believes can only be attained through an endless cycle of constructive criticism.

I look down at my now-empty bowl of pasta, the warmth of my uncle's reunion quickly replaced by the chilling presence of my father.

Jonathan O'Brien has a way of stripping people to their most vulnerable, leaving them exposed like a patient on a hospital bed. Except instead of surgery, where doctors cut people open with the hope of mending, my father simply dissects. He rips open every insecurity, every failure, and lays it bare on the operating table so you can make one of two choices.

Lie there in despair.

Or start reassembling the pieces.

Cody

The most delicious dinner of my life was ruined by the supersized side of fatherly disappointment. Hell, Jonathan O'Brien isn't my father but even *I* felt ashamed of my personal growth these last few months.

Watching him rip apart his children like some judgemental third-party observer was one of the most emotionally draining experiences of my life. It felt wrong on so many levels and that was before Mo elbowed my still-recovering ribs.

My train of thought takes a swan dive when hunger hits my stomach. I check the time and sigh. Almost midnight.

I'm contemplating texting Mo for kitchen directions when a knock sounds quietly at my door. I hop off the king size bed, walking across a bedroom that's bigger than the first floor of my entire house, and open the door.

Stella smirks, "If I'd known you would give me a show, I would have come over sooner."

I put my hands on the doorframe, bare chest and low-slung sweats doing nothing to hide my obvious flexing.

"Just trying to earn my keep."

"And you are doing a marvellous job of it." Stella licks her lips, and the action goes straight to my groin. Quickly dropping my hands, I clear my throat.

Just friends just friends just friends.

"What do you need, Stel?"

I keep my gaze trained on her face, steering clear of the bare legs peeking out of her loose pyjama shorts.

"Figured someone should give you the grand tour."

My stomach lets out an obnoxious growl and her smile grows wider, "Start with the kitchen, shall we?"

"You realize it's almost midnight, right?"

Stella gasps, "Midnight? That's past your bedtime, Ellsworth. Guess I'd better let you get some beauty sleep. See you in the morning!"

She pivots and starts walking away.

I groan, "Stel, wait. Let me just grab a shirt."

"Now *that* is a shame."

"To your left we have my father's sad idea of what an art collection is." Stella waves towards the hideous paintings lining the west side of the East Wing.

Confusing, I know.

"Some of them are nice."

Stella shoots me a look, "Don't lie to me, Captain. I'm not an art expert by any means but even I can tell these are terrible."

"I mean, they aren't that bad..."

Her glare has me laughing.

"You're right, they're terrible. How much did he pay for this one?" I point to a particularly ugly white canvas that has red arrows pointing in every direction.

Stella claps her hands, "I love this game. Guess."

"Uh... five hundred?"

"Cody, nothing in this room is under ten grand. Up your guess."

Ten grand?

My left eye starts to twitch as I do a quick calculation of the dozen or so art pieces scattered around the room.

"Uh... twelve grand?"

Stella smirks, "Fifty."

"Grand?" Disbelief oozes through my tone as I stare at a picture of red arrows that costs more than my annual mortgage.

Holy shit.

She laughs and skips down the hall, making me break into a jog to catch up. We play this game for the next few minutes, Stella pointing at random art pieces and me failing spectacularly at guessing anywhere close to the right price.

We eventually reach the end of the hallway, coming to a stop in front of a photograph set in a simple black frame. It's a picture of the Vancouver skyline, right along the edge of the marina. It's the least extravagant piece we've seen tonight but it's the only one hanging on this wall.

"You know the drill. How much?"

I take my time, calculating the average of the other pieces and considering the simple elegance this one has that all the others lacked.

"Two hundred and fifty." It's on the lower end of the average, but there's something authentic about this one that screams quality.

"Zero." Stella responds after a pause, making me thing she's joking.

"You mean how many zeros?"

"No, I mean it didn't cost anything." She pauses again, studying the one and only piece I could afford in this entire room.

"My mother took the photograph. On their first date." The corners of Stella's mouth tug up in a sad smile, "She had it framed as a wedding gift."

Raising her hand, Stella lightly traces over the blurred corner at the bottom, "That's my father's shoulder. The story goes, he went in for the goodnight kiss but ended up missing because my mother was too caught up trying to take the photo."

She laughs softly, "My mother used to say she fell in love twice that night, first with the city and then with my father."

"Was he different back then?"

I step closer, my feet sinking soundlessly into the plush carpet. Stella turns so we're chest-to-chest, tilting her head to look at me. Her hair hangs loose around her face, the braid from earlier leaving the strands soft and wavy.

My chest constricts as I take in the delicate lashes framing her dark blue eyes.

Her mother's photograph isn't the only priceless thing in this room.

Stella sighs, "In a way. My mother brought out a different side of him. Not softer but... less harsh, I guess? He never stopped smiling around her. Even when they were arguing, my father would get this smile on his face, one that seemed to say he has never been happier."

She smiles sheepishly, "That probably sounds dumb."

I shake my head, "That makes perfect sense. He was a happy man."

"Exactly. He was just as strict, but my mother was his counter-balance. She made sure we had equal amounts of discipline and fun growing up."

A strand of hair falls in her eyes. Without thinking, I reach out and gently tuck it back behind her ear.

"I wish I could have met her."

Stella's breath catches and suddenly, I'm worried I have over-stepped.

"I wish you could have met her too."

She smiles, pressing her cheek into the palm of my hand. The tenderness in her expression has my chest tightening, the magnetic pull between us growing stronger. I gently pull my hand back as a sliver of moonlight creeps through the stained-glass windows lining the opposite wall, casting a rose glow around us.

We stand like that, trapped in a touchless embrace for an indefinite amount of time. The desire to kiss Stella grows with every passing second but I can see the past and tonight's dinner weighing heavily on her mind.

I've watched Stella physically exert herself to the point of exhaustion every day for the past six months, but tonight I got to peek behind the hard planes of muscle protecting her surface. I got to see beyond the bubbly extravert who drags her roommate to every resident event Taber University has to offer.

I clear my throat, deciding not to disappoint us both by pulling the same stunt as last time, "We should probably head to bed, it's getting late."

An eyebrow quirks up, "Sounds like an invitation, Captain."

That's the second time tonight she's referenced to my varsity title, and I'm starting to like it a little bit too much.

"Separately, O'Brien."

At least for tonight.

Stella rolls her eyes, "Always have to be the responsible one, don't you?"

I huff out a laugh, grabbing her hand and giving it a squeeze, "Someone has to be."

We leave her mother's photograph behind as we head back, hand in hand, to our separate bedrooms.

Chapter 14

♥

Cody

I wake up to the sound of someone banging down my door.

"Ellsworth! What the hell are you doing in there?"

Yanking my legs out of bed, I stumble across the room to open the door. Mo is waiting on the other side, looking like he's about to take part in an Under Armour commercial.

He smirks, glancing down at my black briefs, "I shouldn't have left my change in the car." Unzipping the gym bag slung over his shoulder – Under Armour, of course – he tosses me some clothes.

I blindly catch them, eyes still half-closed from the sleep I was so rudely torn from.

"What time is it?"

"Time for you to be out of bed."

Mo waits while I fumble my way into more sponsored gym wear then throws a pair of brand-new sneakers at my feet.

"I thought you were an early bird like my sister."

I grunt, bending down to slip the shoes on, "Not when it's Christmas break."

"Everyone takes a break during the break. This is the time to get ahead."

Once he's satisfied that I am coherent enough to follow him, Mo turns and marches out of my room.

I fall in step beside him, doing my best to stifle a yawn. My eyes are bleary and probably bloodshot, but Mo's are as bright and clear as the icicles dripping outside.

It's annoying to say the least.

We pass the weight room Stella showed me last night, the "smaller" one of their two gyms she'd said. Her definition of small has some serious misconceptions because the glistening dumbbell racks lining the tasteful navy walls easily put Taber's weight room to shame. The pristine black benches and rubber mats look clean enough to eat food off of, and don't get me started on the row of mirrors lining the far wall.

It's every gym bro's wet dream.

We round another corner, successfully exceeding the mental map I'd made from Stella's tour. At this point in the corridor, Stella and I had gone right, into the East Wing, but Mo takes a sharp left turn and jogs down the set stairs that open up before us.

I quicken my pace to keep up, sneaking curious glances at the two other floors we pass.

"For someone who slept for seven hours, you aren't moving too fast this morning."

Mo's voice is laced with humour, his condescending tone exactly as it was when I was a freshman. I open my mouth to correct him then shut it. I still don't know what time it is but it's probably too early to deal with the fallout of going on a midnight tour with his younger sister.

We approach a beautiful crystal sliding door, the design indecipherable but breathtaking, nonetheless.

"Here we are." Pulling the door open, Mo beckons me inside.

I take one step forward before coming to an abrupt halt when I spy what's inside.

A stadium-sized scoreboard blinking 5:17AM.

And Stella dangling upside down, midair, in the middle of the room.

Mo chuckles, brushing past me, "Close your mouth, Ellsworth. It takes away from the jawline."

I snap my mouth shut, mind struggling to process what is being laid out in front of me. Stella wasn't kidding when she said the other gym was small, this gym could easily fit four of those inside and still have room leftover.

"What is she doing?" My eyes haven't strayed from the small frame hanging wrong-side-up off one of the many ropes dangling from the ceiling.

That's right, I said ropes plural. An entire section of the O'Brien's fitness arena is allocated for ropes and rings. There's another section that seems to be made completely of trampolines.

It's like the freaking Olympics.

"She's rope climbing. Without using her legs." Mo shrugs casually, "She's still working on mastering the L-sit rope climb. Going upside down helps keep the pressure on your arms and less on your core."

I watch in amazement as Stella inches her way up the rope. Her platinum topknot remains stubbornly intact in the precarious position.

"Shouldn't someone spot her?" Pressure builds in my chest as I realize just how far off the ground she is. A fall from that high could be fatal.

Mo shakes his head, "That's what the crash mats are for."

I squint, just barely making out the outline of a thick, black mat covering the otherwise spotless hardwood.

Movement hits my peripheral and I glance over to see none other than Jonathan O'Brien in one of the many squat rack sections. I watch in amazement as he loads up a barbell with more weight than I've ever lifted, but before I can watch the execution, Mo claps my shoulder and leads me the other way.

"Alright Ellsworth, time to put your recovery to the test."

We wander closer to Stella, who finally reached the top, and is making her way back down the rope. I breathe a sigh of relief when her feet finally reach the ground, her bright red face throwing me a smile as we walk by.

"What do you have in mind?"

I'm not one to back away from a challenge, but I'll admit there's some trepidation in my voice. Mo might not be a cardio nut like his sister, but that doesn't mean his workouts are any less brutal. They just hurt in a different way.

He shoots me a grin and I bite back a groan.

We stopped in front of the battle ropes.

Stella

Inhale.... Exhale...

The humid air of the sauna coats my lungs in a warm blanket, my body sagging with exhaustion. Sweat drips from my nose onto my extended thigh, and I watch the droplet make a lazy trail down my bare leg.

I breathe through the last of my stretches, the ache of hunger sinking in. I've only been up for a couple of hours, but dinner feels like a lifetime ago.

Quickly grabbing the discarded tank top from the ground, I spring to my feet, the burst of energy in tune with the burst of hunger.

I sigh with pleasure when I push open the door and a rush of cool air hits me.

"Guess it was my turn for the free show." Cody grins, his sweat-soaked shirt plastered to every rigid edge of his chest. He jerks his thumb over his shoulder, "Mo sent me to grab you to go get breakfast..."

I'm so distracted by the wet t-shirt that it takes me a moment to realize Cody's smile has slipped from his face and the teasing glint has disappeared from his gaze. He takes a step closer, his eyes trained on my bare torso.

"What happened?"

I freeze, realizing my tank top is still in my hands and not on my body. My tattoo and my scar are on full display.

He swallows thickly as he takes another step forward, "What happened, Stel?"

The pressure builds in my chest until it feels like I'm back in the sauna and my lungs can't take in enough air.

"My mother was killed in a car crash."

Cody's eyes flick to my face, and I can see the understanding dawning.

"You were in the car."

I nod, dropping my gaze to the ground. I hate seeing people's pity.

"We got run off the road by a drunk driver. Mom died of internal bleeding, I got away with a few stitches."

I can feel Cody's stare, but I refuse to look up. There is one person in this world I do not want sympathy from and that is Taber's lacrosse captain.

"I think it was more than a few stitches." His voice is soft, like he's scared I'm going to flee at any second. Which, for the record, did cross my mind as a viable option.

I force out a painful laugh, "It was just enough to ruin bikinis for me. Anyways, we should probably get going..."

"You don't wear bikinis?"

"I don't know if your vision is intact, but this," I gesture towards the warped skin gracing my side, "Isn't what people want to see when they go to the beach."

My ex-boyfriend taught me that. He couldn't stand the sight of my scar, claimed it turned him off. Said it reminded him of death.

Long story short, we were never going to work out long-term.

Turning so my back is facing Cody, I yank the tank top over my head and tug it past the point of interrogation. He's still staring at me when I turn around, his expression is unreadable.

"You ready for breakfast?" I interject a false brightness to my tone, pretending we didn't just dig up years' worth of grief and physical therapy.

"Yeah."

He falls silent as we head towards the kitchen, climbing back up the stairs to the main floor. A somber mood falls upon us as we walk, side-by-side, with Cody casting the occasional side glance my way. It doesn't take long for me to snap.

"What? If you have something to say, just say it."

I'll admit, my tone tends to grow sharper when I'm uncomfortable. Or hungry.

"It's just…" He frowns, his dirty blonde eyebrows scrunching together, "You shouldn't bottle your grief up like that and you shouldn't hide your scars from the world."

I don't know what I was expecting him to say but it wasn't that.

"That scar is a part of you. It's proof that the O'Brien's never give up, even when your world is torn apart. It shows you're a survivor."

I'm completely speechless but the silence only adds fuel to his motivational delivery.

"You have an amazing body, Stel. It deserves to be shown off." Cody shrugs as if the compliment didn't just set every nerve ending on fire.

"Didn't think you'd noticed, Captain."

"When it comes to you, O'Brien, I notice everything."

Damn it, now I'm grinning like an idiot and Cody is looking pleased with himself. I hate it when men use their charms knowingly.

He clears his throat, "But my point is, you are strong Stella. Strong in the figurative sense as well as the physical. Don't ever forget that."

"I won't."

We end our conversation as we enter the kitchen, Mo and my father already stationed at the dinner table with steaming omelettes in front of them. Cody breaks off to go sit beside Mo, and I head off in search of our personal chef.

My body feels shaky as I request my usual protein shake order, but I can't tell if the shakes are from my workout or the emotional garburator Cody just put me through.

The one thing I do know is it's only been twelve hours since Cody Ellsworth stepped foot inside my house and somehow, he has already taken possession of what's left of my heart.

And it's absolutely terrifying.

Chapter 15

♥

Cody

After the sauna encounter, I don't see Stella for the rest of the week. I'm not saying she went out of her way to avoid me but...

I'm pretty sure she's avoiding me.

"You still snowboard?"

Mo passes me the lacrosse ball with an easy flick of his wrist. I catch it, cradling the red ball in my net as I take a few steps to the left, and pass it back.

We've been training drills for over an hour inside the O'Brien's fitness area, the larger of the two gyms. A gym which, I have yet to see Stella workout in since that first morning.

"Don't get out as much as I'd like but yeah, I still snowboard."

Mo mimics my movements, keeping his steps quick and light before tossing me the ball.

"Perfect. We're going to Whistler tomorrow."

"We?"

"You, me, and Stella."

Mo turns and whips the ball against the wall, the extra force making the rebound soar far above my head. I turn and start running for the ball, knowing full well Taber's all-star forward will come barreling down on me at any second.

I pick up the pace as Mo's footsteps grow louder, my heavy breathing growing ragged as the ball draws near. I'm about two feet from the ball when a brutal shoulder check sends me flying.

"Son of a..." I bite back a curse as I hit the ground, the jarring impact sending a sharp pain through my ribs. I roll onto my back, the cold hardwood doing nothing for my now-aching body.

I hear Mo chuckle as his Vancouver Canucks jersey comes into view.

"Between the two of us, I'm supposed to be the old man."

"Asshole."

He chuckles some more, offering a hand and pulling me to my feet. The smirk on his face is the same one I used to see every practice, as is the familiar urge to slap it away. A prick of nostalgia runs through me and suddenly the weight of these past few months comes crashing down on me.

"I've missed you, Mo. The team doesn't feel the same without you."

The truth has my body deflating like a popped balloon.

Besides getting injured and having my players threaten to forfeit out of loyalty, the only thing I've brought to the team is a tournament upset with our rivals, the Silverwood Sabers. We aren't out of the running for the championship banner, but we're a hell of a lot farther than we should be.

Mo sighs, running a hand through his hair. The impeccably gelled strands don't move an inch.

"I miss being part of the team. The camaraderie, the shit-talking, the pre-tournament anxiety, all of it."

He shakes his head, gently twirling the lacrosse stick between his fingers, "Jonathan has me climbing the corporate ladder. It's okay, I guess. Board meetings are hell, but the income is respectable."

I study my mentor, noticing the dark groves under his eyes for the first time. It's the only imperfection on the guy's face, but it's enough to show he's human.

"Have you ever thought about working elsewhere? You could be Taber's one and only head coach."

I say the last part as a joke, partly because there's no way Mo would ever settle for the measly income he would no doubt receive, but also because it's impossible to see Mo uprooting his life to move back to Taber. He enjoyed his time there, but he also made it very clear he was never coming back.

Too much of a small town, too many familiar faces he used to say.

"Father would never allow it. And if he cut me off..." Mo shrugs, raw honesty washing through his features, "I wouldn't have the means to support myself. Not right now, anyways."

I nod in understanding. When it comes to wealth, I didn't have a quarter of the funds Mo grew up with, but I do know what it's like to stay at a job because it's the only way to gain enough freedom to be who you want to be.

"That's tough."

"Yeah."

The start of a smile flickers across his face, "How are you liking being captain?"

"It's hard."

Mo throws his head back and laughs, the booming sound echoing around the empty gym, "Not all it's cracked up to be, is it?"

I glare, feeling more insulted by the second, "I mean, it's rewarding but it's a lot for one person to take on. Especially when there's no coaches to take on some of the training."

That's the one downfall with Taber University: there are no head or assistant coaches. It's far from university standard, but after some serious budget cuts a few years back, the university had to choose to either cut the team or reduce the supporting staff. And given the sad number of varsity teams Taber already had, the decision was easy.

The downfall is whoever becomes captain has to double as both teammate and coach on and off the field. That means hours spent creating workouts and planning practices in addition to being the leader and role model for all the new rookies.

It's a lot for anyone to handle, never mind a full-time student.

"Do you think it's worth it?"

The question feels like some sort of test, but all that's reflected back at me is genuine curiosity.

"Some days. Others... I'm not so sure."

I expect the honesty to disappoint Mo, but he surprises me by nodding.

"There's more to life than being a varsity captain. Hell, there's more to life than being a varsity athlete. Just the time commitment is a bigger sacrifice than most people realize."

He's right, and the ugly truth is I'm burnt out.

"Do you regret being captain?"

Mo straightens, giving him an extra four inches on me, "I don't believe in regrets. But if I were to redo my university experience there are some parts of myself that I would explore more. And to do that, I would have needed more free time than the position of varsity captain allowed. So, no, I don't regret being captain, but given the chance, I wouldn't do it again."

I mull over his words, "What parts would you explore? I feel like you managed to do things most guys only dream of doing."

That's not an exaggeration, Mo has an entire wall of signed conquests, and most of those came in pairs. When it came to spending his limited free time, Mo made sure he checked all the boxes on female anatomy.

"Just getting to know myself more. I got so focused on becoming the person my father and my team expected me to be, that I didn't get the chance to be who I wanted to be."

"Who do you want to be?"

Mo grins, "Don't get all introspective with me, Ellsworth. You haven't offered any insights into your own dilemma."

I groan, "Because there is no dilemma, I'm just being dramatic. But it's nice to dream about the things I would do with free time."

I immediately think of Stella, of taking her on dates and getting to know each other the way real couples do. Our early morning gym sessions wouldn't have to be the only stolen moments we find together, and we wouldn't have to make an excuse to talk to each other at a house party.

We would simply attend events together.

And spend an entire weekend in bed just because we can.

My train of thought must have been written all over my face because Mo looks at me with a knowing smile, "I think you mean, all the girls you would do with some free time."

I huff out a laugh and quickly look away, "Something like that."

Stella

Incoming Facetime Call...

"Stella!" Lou's smiling face fills my screen and I find myself bursting with excitement. These catch-up calls have kept me going all week and today is no exception.

"My darling Lou, what dirty details have you got for me today?"

A laugh echoes off-screen, causing Lou to glance up and blush deep red.

I try and fail to hold back my smile, "Tell Wes I say hi."

"Wes says hi back!" A male voice shouts the response, making me burst out laughing. Lou's eyebrows pinch together as she scolds her boyfriend lingering somewhere nearby.

"I told you to leave. The door is that way." She juts her chin towards the door, the stern expression betrayed by the smile shining in her eyes.

"But Trip, I want to hear the dirty details. That way I know which moves deserve a repeat performance."

I still can't see him, but I know for a fact Wes is wiggling his eyebrows right now. Lou's exasperated eye roll gives him away.

"Out."

"But *Trip...*"

"Out."

"I love it when you get bossy." The camera shifts so Wes' sparkling green eyes come onto the screen, his wide smile popping out dimples that are dangerous even over facetime.

"Stella, if you hear any sort of complaint, please let me know. My manhood is on the line." He leans back and plants a sloppy kiss on Lou's forehead.

"Make sure you tell her about the hot tub."

Lou's blush returns as her boyfriend leaves, the shy smile on her face putting a happy one on my own. Nothing beats having your best friend in love.

"A hot tub, eh?"

"It was crazy, Stella. We could have been kicked out." Lou's eyes glow in a way that says she's getting good, consistent sex. "It was so much fun."

I pout, "That's all I'm getting? But *Trip...*"

Lou shakes her head, giggling at my spot-on imitation of Wes, "Okay, okay. Long story short, Wes tried to take me skiing yesterday. It was a disaster."

I wince, picturing my uncoordinated roommate on skis. God bless the girl, she can play the air guitar like the best of them, but when it comes to moving her body in any sort of synchronized fashion – it's best to duck and cover.

"After the second run ended with me in tears, Wes decided we should call it a day. He paid for a day room at this ski chalet, and each room had a hot tub on the balcony. If anyone had been staying next door, we would have been arrested for public indecency for sure."

I impatiently wave my hand for her to get to the fun part.

"Anyways, Wes iced my hip for the better part of an hour before he finally cleared me well enough to go in the hot tub." Lou pauses to roll her eyes, "He's so ridiculous sometimes. I only cried because I couldn't remember how to stop and was worried about hurting someone. He thought it was from the fourteen falls I took coming down."

I mean, fair assumption on the man's part.

"But back in the hot tub..." I prompt her with an encouraging smile.

"Back in the hot tub... things got heated." Lou grins at her own pun while I groan.

"So, yeah. We kind of started making out, and then I was on his lap, and then my bikini got thrown over the balcony – which was super embarrassing to go retrieve later by the way – and then he carried me inside to test out the stability of all the horizontal surfaces."

I sigh, "Not nearly as much detail as I would like but that will suffice, thank you."

"You know, if you made a move on Caveman Cody, you wouldn't have to live through my stories."

"Pfft, I'd still want to hear your stories even if I was getting dick left, right, and centre."

"Now there's an image I will never be able to erase from my mind." The deep voice makes me scream and drop my phone.

"What the hell, Mo!"

I hold a hand to my heart, the pulse pounding beneath my fingers. Lou's confused face looks up at me from the floor and I quickly bend to retrieve her.

"Sorry, my brother forgot how to knock. Give me two minutes."

She nods and I quickly mute her. Mo smirks, leaning his large frame against my open bedroom door.

Damn it. I must have forgotten to close it.

"What can I do for you, brother?"

"Well, I'm taking Cody to get fitted for some new boots for Whistler tomorrow and was wondering if there is anything you need."

"Nope, I think I'm good." I pause, unsure of how to ask the question that's been bothering me all week.

"Why didn't you ever tell Cody about our family? About mom?"

Mo tilts his head, taking a moment to think about my question. It's one of my favourite things about my brother: he always takes time to think about his answer.

He might be a dick 99 percent of the time, but he's a well-thought-out dick.

"By the time Ellsworth came into my life, mom had been gone for over a year. When I wasn't playing lacrosse, I was partying myself into oblivion. It was the only way to keep her off my mind. The last thing I wanted to do was talk about the feelings I was trying so hard to bury inside."

"You weren't alone, you know."

"I know. But I had to be there for you too." Mo sighs, "I didn't mean to keep it from him, but I never expected us to grow that close. And once that happened, there was just never a right time to bring it up."

"Cody's got a way of sneaking under your skin, huh?"

Mo chuckles, "You've got no idea."

Oh, but I think I do.

"Anyways, I better let you get back to Lou. See you later." He pushes off the wall and gently closes my door behind him.

"Does this mean you're going to be on the lookout for hot tubs tomorrow?" Lou's voice crackles through my phone the second I press unmute.

"Considering I've avoided the man all week, no, probably not."

"Could be a good way to reunite?"

"It's a nice thought but my brother will be there. Plus, I tend to get a little competitive when it comes to skiing."

Disbelief fills Lou's expression, "A little?"

"Okay, a lot." I grin, adrenalin already filling my veins at the thought of the O'Brien sibling annual ski race. It has been years since I've lost one, and I'm not about to let the varsity captain steal my title of defending champion.

"Poor Cody. He has no idea what he's signed up for, does he?"

"Absolutely not. And I plan to keep it that way."

Chapter 16

♥

Cody

We pull up to the ski resort just as the cracks of dawn start to appear.

Streaks of red and gold illuminate the sky, a fresh layer of snow glistening along the majestic peaks of Whistler and Blackcomb Mountain. The PEAK 2 PEAK Gondola connects the mountains two-thirds of the way up, giving skiers and snowboarders a greater collection of terrain. Compared to Castle Mountain, the small hill just outside of Lethbridge I grew up snowboarding on, Whistler is a whole different level.

One I am not entirely sure I am ready for.

Stella squeals with excitement as Mo puts the car in park. Even though the chairlifts don't open for another hour, the parking lot is already half full. Long johns of every colour imaginable peek out from car doors as families and groups of friends begin the tedious process of putting on ski gear.

"I can't remember the last time I've been to the mountains." I voice the thought out loud and Stella shoots her brother a concerned glance.

She shifts in her seat to face me, "You can snowboard, right?"

I nod, deadpan, "There's never been a run I'm not comfortable sitting down on."

"Oh my god. You're a butt dragger?" Stella's horrified expression is almost enough to break my straight face.

"You know what they say, low and slow is the way to go."

Mo chuckles from the driver's seat and receives a glare strong enough to melt the snow crystals outside.

"This isn't funny."

"It's a little funny."

Stella huffs, flopping herself back against the leather seat, which thankfully did not get pushed back all the way this morning.

"I hate you both."

Mo grins at me in the review mirror and a flicker of excitement kindles inside of me.

The day goes by in a blur of wind-bitten cheeks and fresh tracks. Instead of stopping for lunch, we decide to eat our packed sandwiches in the gondola and maximize the number of runs we hit today. I'm the only snowboarder in our trio, but Stella and Mo remained surprisingly patient every time I had to clip back in after riding the chairlift.

On Stella's part, I think she was just relieved my skills were good enough to keep up with the aggressive terrain the sibling pair loved to attack.

Unused to the deeper powder and longer runs, my legs started to burn two hours ago, but the O'Brien's have yet to show any sign of slowing down. I will be surprised if I can walk tonight, never mind getting out of bed tomorrow.

We slide off the Olympic chair just as a sign goes up signaling last call of the day. I send up a silent prayer of thanks for the early closing time and follow Stella's pink puff jacket off to the side.

I flop down, quickly buckling in my boots as Stella uses one of her poles to draw a diagram in the snow.

"Alright boys, listen up. This year's race is going to be down the lift line, making it easy for the rookie," She nods her equally bright helmet in my direction, "To stay on course. Rules are simple: Whoever gets to the bottom first wins. Sabotage and shortcuts are welcome as long as the Olympic chair remains in your line of sight. Are there any questions?"

I raise a gloved hand.

"Could I get a five-minute head start since I'm the only one who doesn't know the terrain?"

"No. Any other questions?"

My hand goes back up.

Stella sighs, "Yes, Cody?"

"Are you sure about the head start?"

"Positive."

Mo smirks as I lower my hand. With his helmet and goggles on, Mo bears a striking resemblance to his father with his wide and intimidating build. The sleek material of Mo's black Arcteryx coat stretches tight along his shoulders, making the guy look built even under layers of ski gear.

Stella, on the other hand, looks like a cotton candy machine exploded and buried her under layers of pink fluff.

"The trick is to straight line it. Don't think, just go." Mo shrugs casually, as if his suggestion wasn't borderline suicidal.

"What do you mean by straight line? Like don't turn?"

The question sounds stupid even to my own ears, but I want to make sure I understand him correctly. Because the last time I checked, letting my board run free down the side of a mountain is not a recipe for success.

Stella pushes her goggles up on her forehead and gives me a smile. Platinum wisps fly across her face, the loose strands coated in a thin layer of ice.

"He means just go as fast as you can. Mo and I have a bad habit of not turning when the race gets tight, but that's probably because we grew up racing." She smirks, her dark blue eyes shining brightly in the cold mountain air.

"You used to race?"

"Pfft, like ten years ago. We were only in the racing program for a couple of years before we veered into backpacking and avalanche training."

I can't remember the last time my odds of winning were so low.

"And you're still not giving me a head start?"

"Come on, Cody. The only way to be the best is to beat the best. And you can't do that with a five-second head start." She gives me a cheerful smile before pushing her goggles back into position, "The loser has to buy a round of hot chocolate."

"What does the winner get?"

Mo grins, flashing a set of perfect teeth, "The only thing that matters in the O'Brien household. Bragging rights."

Stella

"Ready... And go!"

As per tradition, a recruited stranger starts us off to eliminate any possible advantages. The three of us immediately split, Cody making a beeline for the smooth groomed section directly under the chairlift, Mo veering right to avoid a cluster of skiers, and I take a sharp left and disappear into the trees.

Moguls hit my skis at every turn, but years of practice keep my knees soft and bent to absorb the otherwise jarring impact. I use my momentum to pop over a wind lip halfway down, enjoying the fleeting moment of weightlessness as I leave the ground. I land with a light thump, quickly shortening my turns to increase my speed. I glance to the right to confirm the Olympic chair is still in my line of sight and refocus on the slope in front of me.

The discovery of this shortcut was the turning point for me in these races. When it comes to sheer speed, Mo beats me every time thanks to the extra pounds of muscle he's got, and with Cody it would be no different. It took me a while, but once I figured out it was impossible to beat guys twice my size on a straight-away, I started looking for alternative solutions and stumbled upon this shortcut.

Lucky for me, tight tree runs are my specialty. My lack of height and shorter skis make it easier to execute the short, sharp turns needed to maintain a high speed and avoid colliding with a nearby tree. For the last four years, this shortcut has given me the extra boost I need to outski my brother, and today is no exception.

I fly over the last few moguls and pop out between the trees, folding myself into tuck position as my skis carve into the smooth surface of the groomer. Mo's black jacket hits my peripheral, his large frame mirroring mine as we both go barreling towards the finish line.

I curl myself up tighter, willing my body to go faster as Mo starts to close the distance between us. I'm just about to claim my victory when a flash of green catches my eye.

I jerk my skis to a stop when I realize Cody's jacket isn't above his board like it should be. Mo speeds past me with a celebratory holler, but I'm too focused on the snowboarder cartwheeling down the hill to care.

Cody rolls to a stop near a cluster of trees and without thinking, I unclip from my skis and go running towards his unmoving figure.

"CODY!" My scream gets swept away by the wind, my clunky ski boots making me fumble awkwardly as I run towards the fallen varsity player. The terrible memory of last semester's lacrosse tournament crashes through my head and I feel my panic rising.

"Ow."

Cody's goggles are hanging off the back of his helmet, every crevice of his suit filled with snow. I collapse to my knees next to him, holding back the desire to weep as his coherent brown eyes meet mine.

"Did I win?" His voice is weak but steady, a positive sign he wasn't hurt too badly.

Yanking off my gloves, I cradle his face with my heads and gently wipe away the clumps of snow sticking to his helmet.

"No, you idiot. You were supposed to *snowboard* down the hill, not tomahawk your way down."

He chuckles, bringing his gloved hand up to cup my bare one, "Mo should have clarified the definition of a straight line."

"You need to be more careful, Cody. You're still in recovery."

"I think I'm going to need recovery after this."

Exhaling heavily, I tilt my head back and close my eyes, letting the falling snow melt away the worry circulating inside of me.

"You are going to be the death of me."

"Stel." He tugs my hand, bringing my focus back to his smiling face, "I am completely fine. It was just a fall."

Pushing himself upright, Cody shifts closer, slowly raising a gloved hand to move aside the frozen strands peeking out the sides of my helmet. He uses the other hand to unclip his helmet, letting it fall to the ground before bringing his lips to mine.

Melted snow leaves his lips cold and damp as they press against mine, soft and reassuring as he tugs me closer. I don't notice Cody unclipping my helmet until it falls to the ground and a breeze brushes my hair.

He coaxes my mouth open, and I let him, gently moaning when his tongue snakes out to trace the seam of my bottom lip.

Time seems to slow as I deepen the kiss, my frozen fingers raking through his matted hair. Cody groans and pulls his arms tighter around me. The thick sleeves of his winter jacket do nothing to stop the heat radiating off of him, and I'm about two seconds from ripping away the layers separating us when Mo's voice echoes in the distance.

"STELLA! ELLSWORTH!"

We break apart, breathing heavily. Our puffs of air are visible in the cold air but all I can see is the desire burning in Cody's eyes.

"There you guys are. What the hell happened?" Mo's footsteps draw near, and I sit back on my knees, watching Cody struggle to stand up in the deep snow.

"I ate shit. Multiple times."

More snow falls from his jacket and snow pants when he finally makes it to his feet.

"Tell me you didn't lose your helmet on the way down." Mo's expression turns concerned when he takes in the chaotic state of Cody's hair.

"Nah, I just unclipped it to get some fresh air."

"Good. A concussion is the last thing you need right now." Mo shakes his head, and I take the opportunity to yank my own helmet back on.

"You need help getting down?" Mo looks dubiously at the snow-covered snowboard.

"I'm good. Will take it nice and slow." Pausing to brush off more snow, Cody shoots us a self-depreciating grin, "Hot chocolate is on me."

Mo opens his mouth to argue but Cody raises his hand.

"Rules are rules. Who won the bragging rights?"

I say, "Mo," just as my brother says, "Stella."

We look at each other, identical smiles spreading across our faces. A situation like this only calls for one thing.

"Guess we're coming back for a tiebreaker."

Cody throws his head back and groans while Mo and I high five each other. Nothing beats a good old fashion sibling competition.

We slowly make our way down the hill, stopping momentarily so Mo can run and retrieve my discarded skis. The second Mo is out of earshot, Cody turns and looks at me with an intensity that burns all the way to my core.

"We need to talk. Come get me tonight?"

I nod, feeling flustered before Cody leans in one last time.

"And take us somewhere we won't be interrupted."

Chapter 17

♥

Cody

She's trying to kill me.

Much later than what can be deemed respectable, I open the door to Mo's younger sister dressed in just a t-shirt.

A very short, very white t-shirt.

"You ready?" Stella's eyes glisten in a way that should have me running for cover. Instead, I leave all rational thought behind and follow her out the door.

Moonlight shines through the floor-to-ceiling windows as we walk along the long corridor, the ethereal light making Stella's long hair glow like a halo. My gaze trails down the braid-free strands, watching the way the soft ends brush gently against the top of her waist. With each step her hips sway from side-to-side, as if Stella can't go a single second without dancing.

We take the same route Mo took me that first morning, except instead of descending two levels, Stella takes a sharp left at the top of the stairs. The scent of chlorine hits me as soon as we approach the stainless-steel door, the extra insolation helping keep the moisture from spreading to other parts of the house.

"Holy shit." I breathe the words as we step inside, the blast of humidity making my jeans uncomfortably warm as Stella sashays her way to the edge of the Olympic sized pool.

The glow of the underwater lights is the only light in the room, making the calm surface of the water look like a wall of glass.

Laughing softly, Stella waves me over. I amble closer, growing uncomfortably aware of the fact Stella's t-shirt has become mostly see-through. My gaze gets caught on the lacy black thong peeking through the thin material and it's all I can do not to stare as I come to a stop beside her.

"Didn't know you were a swimmer." My voice is gruffer than usual, the tightness in my jeans no longer from the humid air around us.

Stella shrugs, "I dabble here and there. Went through a triathlon phase but that was short lived. I hate running."

The adorable scrunch of her nose draws a smile out of me.

"You hate running but you love cardio?" I tilt my head in amusement, "Not sure how that one works, O'Brien."

"Please, cardio circuits and running are two very different things. I'll take five rounds of burpees over half an hour on the treadmill any day."

I chuckle softly, "You would be the only one."

She grins and takes my hand, pulling me down to sit beside her. Her bare legs break the surface with a splash, sending ripples flowing in every direction. I roll up my jeans and join her, hissing out a breath when my feet hit the surface.

"It's freezing."

"You'll get used to it."

Stella shoots me a smile and we fall silent. My hand resting on the ground inches closer towards hers, our fingers naturally intertwining when they make contact.

I study her side profile as she stares across the pool. Stella's face is delicate in the way the rest of her body isn't, her pixie-like features untouched by the hours dedicated to the gym. But just like her brother, I can see shadows of sleepless nights darkening the under bags of Stella's eyes.

"Where did you learn to two-step?" The question jolts me out of my stare.

"My mom taught me. Said every good country boy should know how."

Stella squeezes my hand teasingly, "I didn't know country boys hate wearing cowboy hats."

"Oh, I am far from a cowboy. Mom finally realized that when I got my first mohawk."

Stella gasps, "You remember getting your first mohawk? Oh, let me guess what age." She shifts to look at me, making that damn shirt ride up another inch.

One more and that black lace will be on full display.

I clear my throat, "It's probably older than you're thinking."

She hums, closing her eyes as if the answer is just out of sight.

"Eleven. No, wait. Fifteen."

I open my mouth but Stella waves for me to be quiet.

"I change my mind. It's closer to nine."

I wait patiently, letting her run through every number possible. Finally, Stella exhales, puffing a stray strand from her eyes and giving me a nod.

"I've got it. Thirteen."

"You sure?"

She hesitates before nodding, "I'm sure."

I lean closer, carefully watching her expression as I brush my lips past her cheek to whisper softly in her ear.

"Eighteen."

Stella shivers at my proximity, goosebumps raising along her bare flesh. I'm about to nip the tender skin below her earlobe when she pushes me away with a scowl.

"You cheated."

My jaw drops, "How did I cheat?"

She huffs, crossing her arms, "You made it sound like it happened when you were young."

"Did not."

"Did too."

I mirror her defensive stance, torn between wanting to kiss her until she stops arguing and throwing her in the pool.

"You were the one that wanted to guess."

"That's before I knew you would cheat."

I open my mouth to list all the ways this aggravating girl is wrong when she gives me a devilish grin.

"Just kidding."

I move instinctively, yanking my legs out of the water, and sweeping Stella off the ground. She squeals, kicking her legs like an unhappy bride to be.

"I was just kidding! Put me down, stupid."

I smirk, tightening my grip, "I don't appreciate all the name calling, O'Brien. First, you insult my character by calling me a cheater and now you're attacking my intelligence."

Stella giggles and the sound fills my chest with warmth.

"I am so sorry kind sir, would you please put me down so I can stay dry and warm?"

I look at the big blue eyes shining back at me. The smile on her face is sugary sweet but the glint in her eyes is anything but.

"No."

Stella doesn't get another word in before I jump, taking us both into the pool.

Stella

"Son of a..."

My explicit gets cut off when Cody breaks through the surface. Crystal droplets cling to his blonde hair, the spiky ends pointing up in every direction. The glow from the underwater pod lights make his brown eyes look devasting, the molten colour swirling with mischief as he darts towards me.

"Get away!" I shriek and try to swim in the opposite direction, but Cody's powerful arms cut through the water, grabbing my ankle before I can make my escape.

He tugs me backwards, making my shirt billow around me. Kicking against his hold, I manage to get one foot free and use it to push against his chest, launching me forward while he goes splashing backwards.

I'm laughing so hard I can barely breathe as I dash to the closest ladder, grabbing a hold of the rungs and pulling myself out of the water. Just as I'm about to reach land, a pair of callused hands grab my waist and the next thing I know, I'm somersaulting back into the water.

I break the surface with a gasp, sucking down a lungful of oxygen before diving back under. Chemicals burn my eyes as I blink them open, the blurry outline of Cody's jeans making it easy to spot his location.

Using my arms to swim in that direction, I cut a wide path around him, keeping the element of surprise when I push off the tiled floor and fling myself onto Cody's broad back.

"Shit!" Cody stumbles backwards, the momentum from my unexpected koala attack sending him crashing into the water.

"I win!" Clapping my hands with glee, I twirl through the water like a mermaid taking a victory lap.

"Terror."

I laugh, flopping onto my back and kicking my way over to the defeated captain. Cody watches me drift closer, his eyes darkening as they take in the t-shirt plastered to my bare chest.

My nipples were already hard from the cold water, but the heat in his eyes has them aching.

He reaches for me at the same time I reach for him, our bodies coming together as if that's where they were always meant to be. My legs wrap loosely around his waist while my arms drift to his shoulders.

Cody's hands lightly graze my ass before coming to a rest on my lower back. Droplets fall from his eyelashes as he blinks at me.

"Should we talk about that kiss now?"

"Depends on what you have to say." I whisper my answer, scared anything louder might trigger the same reaction as last time.

When I had to watch him walk away.

"I lied."

I blink, "What?"

"I lied." Cody swallows, the action dragging my attention to the scruff on his throat. "I didn't carry you out of that club because I was worried about your safety. I did it because I was jealous."

The fingers pressing against my spine tighten. "I was jealous Hunter was the one who got to kiss you. Hell, I'm jealous of every guy you look at, every guy you talk to."

I smirk, ignoring the way my heart is hammering against my ribcage, "Hayden must have done a number on you."

Cody winces, "About that... I may have purposefully riled you up that morning." I freeze as he hurries to continue, "Watching you go on a date with another guy was agony. I had to make sure it wouldn't happen again."

I try to jerk away but his hold has me trapped, "You tricked me?"

"Let me finish."

"I cannot believe you had the audacity..."

"Stel." Cody takes the risk of removing one hand from my back to cup my cheek.

"Please, just let me finish."

I glare but don't make another move to swim away. Despite my rising frustration, this position is quite comfortable.

"Thank you." He sighs, gently brushing my wet hair back from my face.

"I lied when I said it didn't bother me you were going on a date. When you said yes to Hayden, I wanted to break something. I wanted to fall to my knees and beg for you not to go."

"I lied when you asked why I pretended to be your boyfriend. The reason I couldn't give you a straight answer is because I wasn't pretending. I am crazy about you and that terrifies me." Cody pauses, his gaze flicking to my mouth in memory.

"And lied when I said we could never be together. You're the only person I'd want to pursue something with and that will never change."

I feel tears start to well up, but I blink them away.

"What about my brother?"

Cody sighs, "I'll talk to him. You were right, I was taking the easy way out. I'm willing to fight for you, Stel, I'm willing to fight for *us*. Even if it means burning bridges along the way."

My excessive blinking fails and tears spill over.

"I lied too."

Cody goes still against me, his sudden silence accentuating the thundering beat of my heart.

"I was always going to wait for you."

Chapter 18

♥

Cody

Somehow, we make it back to Stella's bedroom.

Stella was more than willing to get down and dirty on the pool's spotless tiles, but that wasn't how I wanted our first time to go.

"Hurry up, Cody." Greedy hands pull at my wet t-shirt before I can even close her bedroom door. Stella's gaze is flushed and a little unfocused as she all but drags me to her bed.

"Take a breath, Stel. We've got all night."

She scowls and I laugh, purposefully taking my time stripping off my damp shirt and jeans before crawling across the mattress to join her.

Stella eyes my briefs and the erection tenting the damp material. She's still wearing that white t-shirt, which is completely see-through thanks to our dip in the pool. My dick throbs as I take in the pointed peaks of her nipples, and the lacy black thong that has to go ASAP.

"Arms up, O'Brien."

Hesitation flashes across her face and I immediately pull my hands away.

"What's wrong?" I sit back on my heels suddenly aware she might be feeling pressured. Nausea churns in my gut as I try to meet her downcast eyes.

"I'm sorry, Stel. I shouldn't have assumed we'd... Do you want me to leave?" I hold my breath, hoping I haven't just ruined the beginning of something promising.

"No, it's just..." Stella tugs at her t-shirt, her erect nipples still holding my balls hostage. "It'd probably be easier for you if you just do me from behind."

I blink, my mind struggling to connect the miserable look on her face and the graphic image she just painted.

She frowns, "Why aren't you saying anything?"

Because now I'm picturing taking you from behind.

But why would that be easier for me?

"I'm just confused. Do you not want me to see you come?"

Stella huffs, visibly agitated, "I don't care about that."

I am so lost.

She sighs, "I don't want you to have to look at my scar. You can't see it as well from behind." Tucking a strand of hair behind her ear, she gives me a painful smile, "That's what my ex-boyfriend used to say, anyways."

My breathing comes to a halt as I register her words.

"He told you that?" Stella flinches at my harsh tone.

"Well, yeah. We were together before the accident, so it was a bit of an adjustment afterwards." She shrugs as if it's nothing, but I can see the distress shimmering beneath the surface. "I don't blame him, it's an ugly scar. On the inside and the outside."

I exhale through my nose, willing my temper to calm down. This guy was part of Stella's past, so there's no changing the way he treated her now. All I can do is help her write a better future.

"Lift your arms, Stel."

She blinks in surprise before slowly raising her arms. I grab the damp ends of the material and slowly peel it off her body. Once it passes her head, I toss it to the ground and grab her hand.

"Come with me."

"Pretty sure that's the point." Stella tries for a teasing grin, but her movements are awkward and stiff as I lead her off the bed and into the bathroom. We come to a stop in front of the full-length mirror, both of us staring at each other's reflection.

Our figures merge into one as I step behind her. Stella's eyes flick to her scar, and with a grimace, she twists to shield it from view. Her tattoo blazes a path down her other side, *CONSEQUENCES* screaming out in bold, confident letters.

"Do you want to know what I see?"

She stays silent, her gaze searching mine through the reflection.

"I see a warrior. A beautiful warrior who is even stronger on the inside than she is on the outside." Using my fingers, I gently trace her impressive collection of abdominal muscles. They clench under my touch.

"The thing I admire most is your confidence. You walk as if you own the world, which after seeing the house you grew up in, isn't far from the truth."

Stella laughs softly, her gaze never leaving my wandering fingers.

"This," Keeping my touch featherlight, I trace the misshapen seam of her scar, "Should never take away your confidence. If anything, it should add to it. It's your battle scar, Stel. And all great warriors have them."

Tears glisten in her eyes and I have to swallow the lump in my throat as I lower myself down to press a kiss on the damaged skin.

"You are beautiful, Stella. Every single part of you is beautiful."

A sob rips from her throat as she turns and wraps her arms around me. I pull her close, wishing I could go back in time and erase the pain of the past. Erase the day Stella lost her ability to love every broken piece of herself.

The truth is, we are all broken. Some of us just have scars more visible than others.

Stella

Once my tears dry up, we finally get to the fun part.

I've never understood why girls cry during sex and yet here I am, bawling my eyes out before it even begins.

"Does this mean you won't do me from behind?"

Cody laughs, picking me up and tossing me over his shoulder as we make our way to my bed. Yet again.

"Oh no, we will definitely get to that but not for the first round."

I smile like a love drunk fool, hanging over his shoulder in what seems to be his favourite power move: The Caveman Cody Signature.

Tossing me on the bed, he doesn't give me a chance to catch my breath before his mouth claims mine, kissing away any residing doubts about my scar.

I wrap my legs around his waist, pulling the weight of his body on top of mine. We both groan when his shaft rubs against my centre, my panties already soaked. I tug impatiently at his shoulder and without saying a word, Cody understands what I'm asking for. He rolls onto his back, keeping our lips locked as I straddle him.

"Fuck." He breathes the word against my lips, gripping my waist as I grind against him. I trail my lips down his neck, pausing for a quick bite on my journey down.

He jerks in surprise, laughter rumbling through his chest, "I didn't have you pinned for a vampire but that explains a lot."

"What did we say about name calling?" I bite him again, enjoying the way we're still bickering like normal. "Don't make me punish you, Captain."

Cody groans, running his hands up my torso without disgust, "Keep calling me that and this will be over really quickly."

"Promises, promises." I head south from his neck, using my tongue to trace a trail down the rigid lines of his chest. My hand creeps inside his boxers, giving him a playful tug that has him almost falling off the bed.

"Goddamn it, Stella. Let me have a turn."

I smirk, "What was it you said before throwing me in the pool? No."

"I technically didn't throw you in the pool, I *jumped* in..." Cody's mouth snaps shut as I slide off his briefs and take him in my mouth. One long suck from base to tip and he looks ready to burst.

I draw his cock out of my mouth with a pop, "Permission to proceed, Captain?"

Cody grits his teeth and gives me a jerky nod.

I grin, enjoying this power dynamic immensely, "What was that? Couldn't hear you from way down here."

He meets my grin with a glare that's borderline feral. I give his dick an encouraging lick, maintaining eye contact the entire time.

"Is that a yes?"

He growls, "Suck me like you mean it, Stel."

There's not much else to say except Captain's orders.

Torturing Cody was my best idea until it was my turn to be in the hot seat. And then it became my worst.

Karma really is a bitch.

I squirm, my legs trapped under Cody's arms, his head buried between my legs. I say buried, except the varsity player has yet to find the correct spot to dig.

"If you need a map to my clit, I'm happy to give you one."

He ignores me, continuing to lick every spot except the one I want him to.

The man is a sadist.

I shudder as his scruff brushes against the inside of my thigh, the sensation bringing on a new wave of wetness. At this point, my pending orgasm is going to expire before Cody makes his move.

Sensing my impatience, Cody flicks his eyes up with a smirk, watching my reaction as he slides a finger inside of me. My back arches, the need for more overpowering any other sensation.

"Ellsworth. Enough messing around. Can you just..."

I gasp as another finger slips inside, his teeth catching a hold of my clit. *Finally.*

My fingers grip the sheets as his tongue replaces his fingers, the rough stroke bringing me closer to the edge until another insert of his finger pushes me over. Stars hit my vision as pleasure takes over, my body trembling as it comes down from the high.

Once I'm firmly back on Earth, I look down to find Cody watching me with a grin, "Ready to continue?"

"Please. Don't wait on my end."

Taking his time, Cody kisses his way back up my body, his touch delicate as his lips skim the bumpy edge of my scar tissue. Tears threaten to make a reappearance as I watch him worship my body, not showing the slightest hint of disgust at the grotesque mark left by my past.

"Am I hurting you?" Cody pauses, his concerned gaze flicking over my face.

"No. Just the opposite."

I thread my fingers through his hair and tug him back up to my mouth, silently thanking him with my kiss. He responds in earnest, nipping my bottom lip and drawing a whimper from my throat. I arch against him, my aching nipples pressing against his chest.

"Condom. In the nightstand."

Cody's bodyweight disappears for a few painful seconds before he's back on top of me, hastily ripping open the wrapper and rolling the rubber on. I moan when his tip hits my centre, our bodies lining up perfectly.

"Is this okay?" His breathing is laboured, the bulging veins of his arms giving away the control he's fighting to maintain.

I smirk, running my hands up those impressive arms, "A little deeper would be preferred."

My smirk quickly turns into a gasp when he pushes all the way inside, stretching me to the fullest. We both groan when he starts to move, the friction making my legs widen further. My nails dig into his back as his thrusts get faster, pushing me closer to my second climax of the night. Just as I'm about to go over, Cody pulls out and hooks my legs over his shoulder.

He slams back into me, barely giving me time to appreciate the new position before I'm falling apart all over again. Cody keeps going through my orgasm, pushing my own further until he finally reaches his own.

With a groan, he collapses next to me.

"Not bad for a freshman."

I laugh, rolling onto my side to look at him. "Back at cha, rookie."

Cody chuckles, opening his arm for me to scooch closer. I curl into him, our legs loosely intertwining as I use his arm as a pillow. He smiles at me, and I can't help but think his eyes seem softer, as if some of the weight he's been carrying around has finally fallen from his shoulders.

I reach out to wipe a thin layer of perspiration from his forehead. "Think how good your stamina would be if you did my cardio circuits."

An amused eyebrow goes up, "Not sure endless rounds of burpees is going to improve my bedroom performance."

"Well, you know what they say."

"What goes up must come down?"

I grin, "Practice makes perfect."

And because Cody is a very dedicated varsity athlete, we spend the next few hours mastering our technique.

Chapter 19

Cody

I wake up to the sound of someone choking.

The second I realize Stella's warm body is no longer against me, I'm on my feet in an instant. My eyes take a moment to adjust to the darkness as they do a sweep of the room, coming to a stop on a form huddled on the far edge of the bed.

"Stella?" My feet get tangled in discarded clothes as I make my way over. The frantic breathing starts to slow as I draw closer, a pale and shaky hand waving me away.

"Go back to sleep. It's... it's almost done." Stella's eyes are closed, her voice weak and trembling. Even in the darkness, I can make out the dark groves underneath her eyes.

"Can I do anything to help?"

The mattress dips with my weight as I sit beside her, staying close enough to comfort but far enough that we aren't touching.

Stella shakes her head, "I feel better now. Sorry for waking you."

Pushing off the bed, she walks over to her closet and starts pulling out clothes. I frown, glancing at the time blinking on Stella's alarm clock.

"It's not even 4:30, Stel. Where do you think you're going?"

"The gym."

"We went to bed two hours ago." The furrow between my brow deepens, "And are we not going to talk about the panic attack that just happened?"

Stella smirks from across the room, "Pretty sure we were in bed for a lot longer than two hours, Ellsworth."

"That's not the point, O'Brien." I scrub a hand down my face, wishing my brain cells were more awake for this conversation. "You are deflecting again and that's fine. But you are not going to work out with only two hours of sleep. That's how you get hurt."

Ignoring me, Stella makes a beeline for the bathroom. I race over and plant myself in front of the door.

"If I want to go to the gym, I can go to the gym. It's my life and this is my house." She goes to step around me, but I deflect it with a small shift to the left.

"Stel, listen to me. You are exhausted. You are in no shape to push yourself right now."

Stella shoots me a glare that would have lesser men aborting mission.

"Get. Out. Of. My. Way."

I lean down until we're nose-to-nose.

"No."

Her nostrils flare, an angry flush spreading over her features. I watch the frustration make its way down Stella's naked body, her peaked nipples and clenching abdominal muscles momentarily distracting me.

"Come back to bed with me."

My request startles her, so I take the opportunity to press further.

"We'll hit the gym later. Come back to bed, Stel."

Her eyes squeeze shut as she shakes her head, "O'Brien's don't go back to bed. We push through. With no pain there is no improvement."

It sounds as if she's quoting White Goodman from *Dodgeball*, but I know she's just echoing one of the many lessons her father ingrained in her. It wasn't until I met Jonathan that I realized that's where Mo gets it from as well.

"There is no improvement to be made right now. You're not taking the easy way out. You're taking the smart one." I keep my voice soft and gentle, hoping it will soothe the edges of her internal war.

"If I take this morning off, who is to say I won't do it again?"

I smile, leaning forward to brush my lips softly against her forehead.

"Then you would just hit the gym later in the day."

The answer seems so simple, so obvious, but nothing about Stella's past is simple or obvious. I don't know the full extent of Jonathan's do-or-die mentality or how it was passed along but given the automatic response to a panic attack at 4AM is to sweat it out at the gym, I'm thinking there are much bigger issues that need to be addressed.

But not right now.

Gently removing the leggings and tank top from her hands, I let them fall to the floor before steering her back to bed. She follows me silently, climbing back under the covers without a word.

Exhaustion hits me almost immediately, but I fight to keep my eyes open until I see Stella's start to close, her breathing gradually growing deeper.

"I'm sorry, Cody." Her voice is tired and frail, the tone decades older than the girl lying next to me.

"What are you sorry for?"

"For having so much baggage."

By the time I respond, Stella has already fallen back asleep, her head nestled against my chest. I lower my voice to a whisper as I watch the tension seep from her features.

"There's no other baggage I'd rather have."

Stella

"You two fucked."

Mo crosses his arms and gives us one of his infamous death glares. If we weren't related, I can see how that look could be intimidating on a lacrosse field. Think I'm more at risk of frostbite right now than I was on the ski hill yesterday.

Widening my eyes to assume innocence, Cody ruins my strategy by nodding.

"We spent the night together, yes."

Mo flicks his eyes over each of us, his posture as rigid as the granite countertop behind him. "Are you a thing?"

Before Cody can respond, I shake my head. "That's none of your business. And how did you know we had sex?"

Next to me, Cody groans under his breath while Mo huffs out a humourless laugh.

"Besides the fact you both skipped morning workout today? The huge ass hickey on Cody's neck is a bit of a giveaway."

I turn to look at the varsity captain, clapping a hand over my mouth when I see the fist-size purple bruise blooming just above his hoodie. Cody smirks and mouths *vampire* at me.

"You should have said something!" I start to giggle despite the murderous look Mo shoots my way, "I would have gone easier on you this morning."

Cody shrugs, "I enjoyed how much you enjoyed it."

"Jesus Christ." Mo presses his palms into his eyelids, exhaling heavily, "Enough with the visuals."

Cody chuckles and it seems to ease some of the tension from the room. The moment temporarily rekindles some of their bromance until my brother switches back to the protective older brother mode.

Otherwise known as The Dick.

"What are your intentions with my sister?" I roll my eyes at the cliché, tugging Cody's hand to lead him away from the interrogation.

"Well…" Cody's eyes flick to mine and the flash of hesitation brings on a wave of nausea. I could blame it on the lack of sleep, but we all know that would be a lie.

"You don't have to answer that." My response is steady and firm, the polar opposite of how I'm feeling inside.

I would never expect Cody to get down on one knee after spending one night together, but I really do think we have something special. Something that is more than just a hookup. Something that could withstand my never-ending list of buried vulnerabilities.

I am crazy about you and that terrifies me.

Cody's pool-bound confession echoes through my mind and I grasp at it, seeking reassurance in a situation that is anything but reassuring.

"Stella, could you give Cody and me a moment? There are some things we need to discuss." The underlining *man-to-man* nearly has me rolling my eyes again, but I refrain, not wanting to steal Lou's signature reaction.

"Considering I am 50 percent of this situation I feel it's only fair I get a say in whatever goes on here."

Mo sighs, "Stella, don't be difficult. Give me two minutes to talk to Ellsworth and if I'm happy with his response, then he's all yours."

"If you're happy with his responses? Since when do the guys who date me need to pass an interview?"

Cody clears his throat and I blush, realizing the slip-up.

"I mean, the guys who have the potential to date me. The ones who might be interested." My face is getting hotter the more I stammer, so I change tactics. "Whatever! You both know what I'm trying to say here."

Not my smoothest comeback, but it broke the cycle.

"Stel." Cody gives my hand a squeeze, "Give me two minutes with Mo. He deserves an explanation."

"Does my explanation not count for anything?"

Cody's mouth quirks up in the smallest smile, "It counts for everything. But right now, this is about me breaking his trust, and that's something I have to face on my own."

I huff, "You are both misogynistic idiots." Turning on my heel, I stomp from the room and throw one last comment over my shoulder.

"Cody better not come back with a black eye."

Their voices fade as I leave the kitchen, my angry footsteps getting swallowed up by the lush carpet in the corridor. I reach my bedroom door, but my irritation has me feeling restless enough to keep going until I reach Mo's bedroom on the same floor.

While my bedroom was more Barbie Dreamhouse inspired, Mo's was inspired by the ocean. His childhood was consumed with week-end sailing trips with my father, and his bedroom walls reflected that.

Pushing open the door, I'm surprised to see sailors and seagulls still gracing the walls. Mo's bedroom looks identical to the one from my memories, and for a moment, it feels as though I stepped into a time capsule.

"Come on, Stella!" Mo's grinning face twirls by mine as he follows mother around the dinner table. Mother laughs, swinging her hips to the music pounding through the speakers, cheering on an 8-year-old Mo as he climbs onto the table for a solo.

"No fair!" Immediately racing for a chair to climb up on, I scramble up next to my brother.

"Get down from there." Father's deep voice breaks through the music, causing both Mo and I to freeze mid tabletop performance.

Mother laughs, "Let them be, Jonathan. They're just having fun." The scowl drops from his face as she shimmies over and loops her arms around his neck.

"Dance with me handsome."

Father's entire demeanour changes as he smiles, taking mother's hand and stepping in time to the music.

"How is it every time I come home from work, you three are always dancing?"

Mother grins and pulls father towards the dinner table. "Everything is better when you're dancing. That's just a fact of life."

Mo and I clap and cheer as mother joins us on the wooden table. Father shakes his head and watches us with a smile.

Sporadic buzzing pulls me from the past, drawing me closer to the nightstand next to Mo's nautical themed bedspread. Although his décor remains untouched since my mother was alive, the brand-new iPhone and shiny cufflinks strewn across the desk attest to the older version of my brother residing here.

The phone buzzes again, the screen lighting up with a list of notifications. My face is already programmed in Mo's phone for facial recognition, so with a quick swipe of my finger, I'm in.

CARTER: Thanks for last night, we should do that again sometime ;)

BRIAN: Bash going down next Tuesday, you in?

STEPHANIE: I'm going to be in town next week if you're interested...

I smirk, recognizing the name of the girl from the airport. Scrolling down, the list of Mo's conquests is endless, as are the number of party invitations. My father's number pops up a couple of times, but all work related.

Disappointed, I put his phone back down and make myself comfortable on his 4 poster California King bed. When my brother returns from lecturing Cody, he and I are going to have our own little heart-to-heart.

Chapter 20

♥

Cody

"So. You and Stella."

Mo's cold stare sweeps over me, his gaze lingering on my bare feet peeking out of my sweatpants. Probably should have covered up the dogs for this conversation.

"I'm sorry Mo, I really am. I should have talked to you before it got this far."

My first-year mentor pushes off the counter and walks over to where I'm standing. I roll my shoulders back, clench my jaw, and brace myself for the impact.

"What the hell took you so long?"

A hand claps my back, and the shock of it almost sends me flying.

Mo grins, "Easy there, captain. The fact you two have been crushing on each other for months now has been pretty damn obvious. It was about time you made a move."

I regain my balance, struggling to recover my thought process.

"Wait. You're not upset Stella and I got together?"

"That depends," Mo gives me a pointed look, "Does got together mean you *are* together or just having sex?"

Nothing about last night was *just* sex.

"The first one."

"Thought so." Mo nods, satisfied with my answer, "In that case, no I am not upset you two got together. Besides the fact you snuck behind my back to fuck my sister, you're still the most stand-up guy I know."

I wince at the crude language, "Before this trip, we'd only kissed once. I was waiting for the right moment to tell you but then..."

Mo holds up a hand, "One thing led to another. Really don't need to know anything else."

Relief crashes over me as the guilt from these last few months finally falls from my shoulders.

He tilts his head, studying me carefully, "Why didn't you approach me sooner?"

I sigh, "I was scared. You took me under your wing and showed me the ropes to the team and the university. And then you honoured me with the rookie-of-the-year award and nominated me for team captain. The least I could do was look out for your sister like you asked me too. I just didn't expect to develop feelings."

Mo's pale blue eyes soften. "You were in a tough position. I know what it's like to not want to disappoint a role model figure."

I survey the older O'Brien sibling in front of me, Mo's impressive physique and impeccable appearance leaving no hint to what cracks lie underneath.

"What did your mother's death cost you?"

If my question startled Mo, he does a good job of not showing it.

"Freedom."

"Freedom?"

Mo nods, "The day I buried my mother is the day I buried my ability to be anything beyond my father's expectations."

Before I can fully register the meaning behind his words, Mo clears his throat.

"Anyways, with the exception of your sex life try and keep me in the loop moving forward. You can come to me for anything."

"I know. Thank you, Mo."

"Don't thank me. You know what you're signing up for with my sister." He winks, tossing me a picture-perfect apple from the bowl on the kitchen counter.

"Hurry up and eat. I want to kick your ass playing one-on-one again."

I catch the apple, the green surface shiny enough to show my smiling reflection.

"Whatever, old man. You only won because I was taking it easy on you."

Mo raises a disbelieving eyebrow and I give my middle finger.

Stella

The bedroom door opens just in time for the foam bullet to hit my brother right between the eyes.

Bullseye.

From my precarious location, I see Mo do a sweep of the room, looking for my hiding spot. His eyes linger on my usual spot by his closet when I let another shot fly.

Pop! Another head shot to my kill score.

Mo quickly zeroes in on my position with a smirk before walking over and holding out his hand for a weapon.

"Nuh uh. This is an ambush. You don't get to retaliate." I fire off another shot, but he dodges it, jumping onto the bed and snagging the toy gun from my hands.

"Hey!"

Shimmying along Mo's upper bedpost, I swing my legs over the side and throw myself onto the thick navy comforter below. By the time I sit up, Mo has reloaded and is firing shot after shot at me.

I roll along the mattress, foam bullets pelting my back along the way. My feet hit the floor and I dash towards my brother, throwing all my weight against his legs. Mo stumbles and I sweep his legs out from under him, knocking his large frame to the ground.

We wrestle for the toy gun until we are both covered in carpet burns and Mo stands up in victory.

"I win!" Mo grins at me, his chest heaving with exertion.

"But did you see that tackle I made?"

"That was super sweet. My back didn't appreciate it, though."

I wheeze out a laugh, walking over to give my big brother a hug. Mo wraps his arms around me, his signature cologne filling my senses.

"You okay, Stel?"

"He makes me happy, Mo. Happier than I've been in a long time."

Mo sighs, releasing his hold, "That's not what I'm asking."

His gaze searches mine and it finally dawns on me what he's asking.

"I'm hovering around okay. I've been missing mom a lot recently. Starting university without her just feels wrong." My tear ducts start to burn as I think about all the events my mother will never get to hear about.

All the people she will never get to meet.

"I know it's hard." Mo stares at me sadly, his eyes dry as the day he told me my mother was never coming home.

There have always been inequalities between my father's expectations of Mo and me, but thanks to my chromosomes, I managed to skip the lessons on masculinity. My brother and his shrivelled-up tear ducts were not so lucky.

"But I hope you know mom would be proud of you. She would have loved to hear about all the events you drag your shy roommate to and she would have loved to hear about this thing you have with Cody."

I smile, wiping the dampness from my cheeks, "You know me too well. What would you say to mom if she was here?"

Mo goes silent, his throat working up and down.

"I would ask her if she ever wanted to be someone different. If she ever wanted to escape the path laid out in front of her."

I rest a hand on his arm, "Is this about working for the family company?"

Mo shakes his head, "That's only part of it. Lately I've been feeling like I'm living someone else's life."

I frown, unused to seeing my brother so shaken.

"Then why don't you take some time off? Step back and figure out what you really want to do. You always have a choice, you know."

"Look who is giving out the advice now."

"I always give advice. You just always choose to ignore it." Mo chuckles and I give him a gentle shove.

"Pick whatever path you want, Mo. You only get one life, and it could end tomorrow or eighty years from now. May as well make the most of it."

Not our most morbid conversation ever, but definitely ranking in the top ten. When you lose a loved one you start to realize how little time we all really have.

Mo nods, "You've given me lots to think about. Thanks sister."

"Anytime brother."

We smile at each other, and for a moment, I wonder if the thought running through my head is the same one that's running through his.

What would mom think of the people we've become?

Chapter 21

♥

Cody

Incoming Facetime Call...

"MERRY CHRISTMAS!"

My mom's smiling face fills my phone screen, her signature Santa hat standing loud and proud atop her blonde hair.

I grin into the camera, "You're a few days early mom."

She frowns, "Today is December 25th, Cody. Have you been training so hard you forgot?" She squints, peering into the camera, "Where are you?"

It's Christmas already?

"Oh," I turn the camera around to give her a sweep of the guest bedroom. "Mo invited me to stay with his family over the break."

"You mean Mentor Mo?" My mother's eyes widen as she takes in the pristine state of the room, "What a lovely colour. I didn't realize your friend was so affluent."

I nod, admiring the dark green colour decorating the walls, "Me neither. Turns out his father is a bit of an entrepreneur."

"Based on the size of that room, I'd say he's more than a bit of an entrepreneur." She shakes her head with wonder, no doubt picturing the closet-sized office that doubled as a guest bedroom in the house I grew up in.

"Didn't Mo have a younger sister? Sally?"

"You mean Stella." Just saying her name has my chest expanding with pride.

"Stella! That's right. She's a freshman this year, isn't she?"

"Yeah. We've gotten pretty close over the break."

My mother's eyebrow raises knowingly, "Will I be meeting this girl anytime soon?"

"Hopefully." The thought of introducing Stella to my mom already has my face breaking into a cheesy ass grin.

"I see." My mother beams through the screen, her happiness as infectious as ever, "In that case, I cannot wait to meet her."

Her camera jostles and I get a shot of Hank waving from beside a lit-up palm tree.

"Merry Christmas, Cody!"

Choosing not to comment on the fact he is half naked in a set of elf boxers, I wave back with a smile, "Merry Christmas, Hank!"

My mother sighs, "I can't believe you forgot what day it was."

"I've been keeping busy. Must have slipped my mind." I run a hand through my spiked hair, uncomfortably aware the break is quickly coming to an end.

Soon, Stella and I will be going back to school. I'll go back to being a varsity captain and she'll go back to tormenting her roommate with every residence event possible. And we will... what? Go back to being gym buddies? Go on dates when I'm not training, studying, and coaching?

Whose place would we stay at?

A headache starts to form at the back of my skull as the questions of reality come crashing down. This break has been amazing, Stella and I have spent more time together these last few weeks than we have all year, but how will we manage in the real world?

My mother's voice breaks through my spiralling thoughts, pulling me back to present.

"Well, don't go pushing yourself too hard. You'll be back in routine before you know it."

That's what I'm afraid of.

We chat for a few more minutes before ending the call with promises of bringing Stella home soon. My phone pings with a series of incoming texts, confirming my forgetfulness.

Nico: Merry Xmas Sexy.

Mason: Hope you're holed up with a lacrosse bunny somewhere. Happy Christmas Ellsworth.

Wes: Tis the season to feast upon the blood of our enemies – Championship banner here we come! Merry Christmas, Cap.

I smile, typing out replies and sending a few messages of my own. Once I'm finished, I grab my phone from the nightstand and pull up Mo's number.

"You know we are living in the same house." Amusement seeps through his voice, and I can easily picture the smirk on his face.

"I need a favour."

"Shoot."

"Can you drive me to a nearby mall? I need to make a purchase."

Mo chuckles, "That's the easiest favour I've ever had to deliver. Meet me on the driveway in ten."

"Did you know it's Christmas today?"

The Cadillac's engine rumbles as Mo accelerates onto the highway. The black model is identical to the one he was driving back in Taber, making me wonder how many of these the O'Briens have on hand.

"Is it?" Mo shrugs, "Came up fast this year."

I'm stupefied by his reaction. From what I've seen, Mo's family isn't devotedly religious, but even the laxer Christians tend to celebrate the opportunity for a family gathering.

"Does your family not celebrate it?"

"We used to." Another shrug, "It was mom's favourite holiday, so every year she would go all out on decorations, making sure Santa left everyone a surprise under the big family Christmas tree. After she died there just didn't seem to be a reason to celebrate anymore."

I frown, thinking over his response. Most families would have come together after such a terrible loss. The O'Briens used it as an excuse to withdraw from each other even more.

"Does it bother you?"

Mo shoots me a sideways glance, "Does what bother me?"

"The barriers the accident created within your family."

He falls silent, his focus returning to the icy roads ahead. Mo's expression remains detached as he thinks over my comment, like he's a third-party observer rather than one of the affected family members.

It's a little unnerving if I'm being honest.

"It would be nice to see a glimpse of the man my father used to be. Sometimes it feels like we lost both parents in the accident."

I study the hard edge of Mo's profile, his rugged features giving no indication of the emotions buried beneath.

"So, I guess sometimes it bothers me." He shoots me a wry grin, "But really I owe you a thank you."

I blink in surprise, "For asking uncomfortable questions?"

Mo shakes his head, "For bringing back the old Stella. It's been a long time since I have seen her sparkle like she does now."

"Sparkle?" The frivolous word sounds ridiculous coming out of his mouth.

"You know, the exuberant way she tackles life with as much glitter and pizzazz as possible."

I chuckle, "That has nothing to do with me. Your sister's sparkle is one hundred percent her own."

"For sure, but you have helped bring it back. And it's really nice to see."

Touched but unsure of what to say, I fall back against the leather seats. Stella and I have come such a long way, but it feels as though we have a much longer road ahead.

We've spent almost every night together since the pool seduction, which has been beyond amazing, but every morning I wake up to the sound of Stella choking on her past. Besides encouraging her to seek professional help, there is nothing I can do except provide emotional support.

Mo flicks on his indicator, slowing down as the exit for the city centre comes into view.

"It goes without saying what I will do to you if this relationship leaves Stella with a broken heart."

I nod, meeting his hardened gaze, "I would expect nothing less than agony followed by a slow death."

A car honks as we merge into the lane and Mo calmly flips off the driver.

"Always knew you were more than a pretty face, Ellsworth."

Stella

CODY: Where are you?

The second I see his name pop up on my phone, my day feels infinitely times better.

It's pathetic, really.

ME: I could ask you the same thing. You've been MIA all morning.

CODY: Did you miss me?

ME: Not as much as you missed me.

I grin, watching his typing bubbles pop up then disappear. Beating Cody in conversation is almost as satisfying as teasing him in the bedroom.

Almost.

Humming to myself, I kill time waiting for his response by pulling up the photo Lou sent me this morning. It's of her and Wes wearing matching Christmas pyjamas, looking sickeningly adorable with a *Happy Holidays!* sign held up between their smiling faces.

CODY: Come to your bedroom so I can show you how much I missed you.

Now there's an offer any self-respecting woman should never refuse.

I pivot in the hallway, almost crashing into my father as I go running around the corner.

"Stella. You should know better than to run indoors. Watch where you're going." An arm reaches out to steady me as cold blue eyes meet mine.

"Sorry, father. I am late for a date."

Booty-call would be more accurate, but that is one detail I am sure my father could go without. His eyes narrow, taking in my baggy sweatshirt and loose cargo pants.

"You may want to get yourself cleaned up. Your hair has seen better days."

Ouch.

Holding back a grimace, I give the man who funds my lifestyle a tight smile.

"Good idea. I will get right on that." I go to step around him but hesitate when I remember Lou's photo, "Merry Christmas by the way."

Jonathan turns his head sharply, and for a moment, I swear I see a glimmer of regret break through his hardened gaze. But as always, my father choses the safer, more distant route and gives me a stiff nod before continuing down the hall.

Shaking off the disappointment, I return to the mission at hand and make it to my bedroom without any further hallway accidents. There's only one man I want to crash into at this point and I find him waiting for me on my bed with a small white box in his hand.

Wait. Why is there a small white box in his hand?

Trying to absorb the sexy figure lounging on my pink comforter in a plain white t-shirt and black jeans, it takes a second for my brain to connect the festive dots.

"Is that for me?" He nods and I don't bother holding back my squeal of excitment.

Cody chuckles, "Don't get excited until you open it."

I march over and snatch the box from his hands, "You could have gotten me an empty box and I would still be excited. The last Christmas present I opened was wrapped in an obituary and it was incredible."

Cody gives me a confused look and I laugh, "It was from Lou."

"Ah." He nods, no longer needing an explanation.

I gingerly sit next to him on the bed, my hands shaking slightly as I peel off the lid. Up close, the box isn't white but covered in white sparkles, making it look like a layer of fresh snow perfectly glued in place. Baby pink paper tissue greets me when I finally get inside, the meticulous wrapping already bringing tears to my eyes.

For me, presents have never been about the purchase. It's about the thought and effort behind the gesture.

"At this rate, I'm going to die of old age before the big reveal." Cody's breath tickles my ear, his proximity much closer than it was two seconds ago.

I shush him, "Don't rush me. I'm enjoying myself."

"By all means then. Admire the pink paper."

I try for a scowl but end up beaming in his direction, "I will, thank you."

Cody heaves a sigh, flopping down on my bed. The mattress bounces beneath me and I'm suddenly distracted by the sight of his bare torso peeking out beneath his shirt.

He smirks, "Like the view?"

"It would be better if you lost the shirt."

"We'll get to that. Now, can you open the present already? I'm getting nervous." I laugh before realizing Cody actually does look nervous.

Stomach clenching, I turn my attention back to the gift, tugging at the pieces of tape holding it together. Two pieces of material fall into my hands, and I let out a gasp.

"Did you buy me a bikini?"

Cody sits back up and nods with an anxious smile.

"You made it sound like you didn't have one, so I figured it might be a good gift." My heart starts to pound as he continues, "You can practice wearing it around me until you are comfortable enough to wear it out in public, but it's time to show off that body, Stel."

I hold up the bikini, the black zipper and camo print making it look like something G.I. Jane would wear to the beach. Cody moves next to me on the bed, coughing softly into his hand.

"I thought the colour would help show off your warrior side. And make other guys too intimidated to approach you."

I laugh softly, tears silently cascading down my cheeks.

"It is perfect, Cody. It is so perfect." I shift on the bed, turning to bury my face into his neck, "Thank you."

I feel him smile against my shoulder, "Merry Christmas, O'Brien."

"Merry Christmas, Ellsworth."

A feeling of hope blossoms inside me, a feeling I haven't felt since my mother and I got driven off the road by a drunk driver.

I will never be the girl I was before the accident, the one who had a loving mother and a father who loved on occasion. But maybe one day I can become someone who isn't afraid to show her battle scars to the world.

Chapter 22

♥

Cody

I groan as my phone buzzes in my hand.

"Another one?" Stella looks up from her tablet with an amused eyebrow.

"Nico is already planning a post-break party." I mutter the words, silencing my notifications to stop the insistent buzzing of the team group chat.

"Ooh, what's the theme this year?" Stella sits up in her seat, eyes already sparkling with excitement. Mo chuckles from the row in front of us, holding the seat with the best view of the front of the plane.

"Don't let Stella pick the theme, everyone will end up naked and covered in neon paint."

Stella sighs, "That was always my favourite *Teen Wolf* episode." She shoots me a wink, "You always reminded me of the twins."

Completely lost, I look to Mo for help.

He shrugs, "Don't look at me, Jackson was my favourite. He got the hottie."

Stella rolls her eyes, "Of course you liked the character who was the biggest douche."

"He was the best lacrosse player too."

I raise my hand, "Should I take the twins comment as a compliment then?"

The siblings ignore me and continue to bicker about fictional characters I have never heard of. My phone screen lights up once more, silently this time, so I reach over and pull up the thread.

WES: Everything dipped in chocolate.

WES: But like more than just the food.

NICO: That's a terrible idea. Someone is going to take it too far and cover themselves in shit.

HUNTER: Why would someone cover themselves in shit?

NICO: Freshmen are unpredictable. That is all I am going to say on the matter.

WES: BRO remember back in seventh grade?!

NICO: That is exactly what I am referring to.

HUNTER: Wait. That actually happened??

MASON: Oh yeah, I've heard this story.

WES: It was trauma for us all.

I chuckle, unsurprised the planning has been completely sidetracked. Nico and Wes always get the job done, but they tend to do it in the most unconventional and entertaining way possible.

ME: Stella suggested neon paint like something from an old tv show?

MASON: Are you and little O'Brien hanging out during the break?? Brave man.

NICO: OMG. HE MEANS TEEN WOLF!!

WES: We have to. Especially after all the cardio Cap made us do.

ME: Am I the only one who has never seen this show?

HUNTER: Yup.

Small, callused hands brush my neck and I immediately put my phone down. My breath catches as big blue eyes smile at me, making me wonder who I blew in another life to deserve Stella's undivided attention.

"So, I was thinking..."

"A dangerous hobby."

She gives me a stern look, but the smirk tugging her lips tells me a different story. I pull her closer, bringing those snarky lips to mine before she can get another word in.

Stella's squeak of surprise turns into a quiet moan as I tangle my fingers in her hair and take her mouth. Stella's hands run down the front of my shirt, pressing shamelessly against every crevice of my chest.

Nipping her bottom lip, I draw a whimper from her mouth as I deepen the kiss. My hands start to wander south but before I can get too far, a hard smack hits the side of my head.

"Don't push it, Ellsworth."

Stella and I break apart, our breathing heavy as Mo shoots me a filthy look from the row ahead. Removing my hands from Stella's body, I give him an obedient thumbs up before he turns back around and pops some air pods in.

"So, you were thinking?" I bite back a laugh at the dazed look on Stella's face, her hair a complete disaster now that I've had my way with it.

"Uh, right. I was thinking," She pauses to lick her lips, making my eyes drop back down to the glistening colour. "Maybe we should plan what nights to see each other? You know, to make it easier with your training schedule."

It takes my lust-swollen brain a second to catch up.

"You mean plan what nights we sleep together?"

She nods, a faint blush staining her cheeks, "Yeah, I just figure on days you have tournaments or early morning practices you'll want a restful sleep. And you know, not get woken up every morning by my issues."

I frown, "That sounds terrible."

Hurt crosses Stella's face before irritation takes its place, "It was just a suggestion. We can put the sleepovers on hold until after lacrosse season is over."

She goes to move away but I grab her hand and intertwine our fingers.

"That's not what I meant. Spending a single night without you is what sounds terrible. And stop feeling guilty for having struggles. Despite what your father may think, you are only human." I give her fingers a reassuring squeeze, "Your problems are my problems and mine are yours. We take on the skeletons in the closet together."

Stella blinks with surprise, her defensiveness visibly slipping away. "Oh."

Running my thumb along her jawline, I lean forward to plant a soft kiss against her lips.

"You can stay at my house any night of the week. And on the nights you feel like staying at your dorm, I'll come to you."

"Sounds like we're going to be seeing a lot of each other."

"I plan on seeing you as much as our schedules allow it. Once tournaments start up, I'm not going to lie, it's going to be tough. But as long as we keep communication channels open and trust each other, I think we will be just fine."

Stella sighs, "You sound so confident."

"That's because I am. There are a lot of things I'm uncertain about but when it comes to how I feel about you, Stel, there is not a trace of doubt in my mind."

Mo pops out an air pod, "I should be writing this stuff down. You're pretty good at this gushy stuff, Ellsworth."

Stella laughs while I stare at him in horror.

"Were you listening this whole time?"

Mo shrugs, "Couldn't get into my podcast with a love confession going on behind me."

Stella snorts, "You are such an old man."

I groan, leaning my head back against the luxurious leather seat.

"That was supposed to be a private moment, Mo."

"You should be thanking me, now you have someone who witnessed your first moment as a whipped man."

Johnson pipes up from the pilot seat, "From what I've heard, that boy has been whipped long before this flight."

The O'Brien's fall apart laughing while I sigh in defeat.

Stella

"Why is there paint on the floor?"

After giving me an enormous reunited-at-last hug, Lou turns to survey the paint shop that is now our dorm's living room. I grin, gesturing towards the tubs of neon paint like a car salesman presenting his most prized vehicle.

"We've got a party to hit this weekend!"

Lou frowns, "Wes mentioned something about that. But where does the paint come in?"

My beaming smile remains undeterred, "It's a neon party! The lacrosse team is bringing in a blacklight, so the goal is to glow as much as possible."

She frowns, "Don't most people just buy bright clothing from a second-hand store?"

Salesman persona firmly in place, I bend down to peel off the lid of the closest tub and gesture towards the unnatural orange glow.

"Some do, but this is better. Picture the infamous scene from *Teen Wolf*."

Lou blinks at me, "Is that a movie?"

I shake my head solemnly, "No, no it is not."

Popping the lid back into place, I stand up and march towards my room, returning seconds later with my laptop in tow.

"Time to get you up to speed, my dear. You can thank me later."

We watch the twenty-minute segment in complete silence, the cinematic masterpiece of hot bodies covered in neon paint leaving little room for conversation. By the time the clip ends, Lou is holding the necklace Wes got her, a slight flush staining the base of her neck.

"I understand now."

I nod without comment, giving my roommate time to absorb the educational lesson I just gifted to her. She shifts on the dorm's uncomfortable couch to look at me.

"Does this mean Caveman Cody will be your date to the party?"

I smile coyly, "Maybe."

Lou claps her hands with excitement.

"It's about time! Wes and I made bets on when you two would become official."

"I mean, we haven't had the official boyfriend/girlfriend conversation yet..."

Lou's excitement drops noticeably, "Wait. But you are together, right?"

"We are, but we haven't discussed labels or anything. So, depending on the terms of the bet, I don't know if that qualifies."

Lou taps her chin, face pensive, "I said you two would be together before the end of the break, Wes said by the New Year."

"Then tell him we got together over the break. Christmas Day, if you want to get technical about it. That way you win."

"I really don't mind losing." Lou's grey eyes take on a mischief glint that I am proud to say is one hundred percent my influence, "But *technically* that wouldn't be cheating since I got it from the source, so..."

"So, you win fair and square. I can write and sign a statement if you need evidence."

"Nah, Wes will take my word for it. I'm sure he has already hit up Cody for the same information."

I reach over to give my best friend a hug, "God, I missed you over the break. How was meeting the family?"

Lou smiles, "It was really great. Wes' family was so welcoming, and his sister and I really hit it off."

"Lacey, right?"

"That's right. She's coming to Taber next year, actually."

"And how did Christmas with your family go?"

It comes as no surprise to hear Wes managed to charm all the Mackenzies within the short week he was there. I haven't met anyone who matches Wes' level of charisma and charm, never mind his ability to befriend anyone and everyone. Lou's boyfriend might come off as over-the-top dramatic most of the time, but when it comes down to it, he's truly a genuine person beneath all the charades. And in my opinion, that is what drew the two of them together.

A bittersweet pang hits my chest as I listen to Lou's stories of Christmas shenanigans and family meltdowns. Her stories are so full of passion and familial love that it makes me nostalgic for the holidays and mishaps my own family used to have.

"... You should have seen everyone's reactions when Wes mistook Uncle Randy for my infamous Uncle Jamie. Took him over an hour to get back in Randy's good books." I laugh, picturing the scene with ease.

We spend the better part of the next hour catching up, shamelessly (at least on my end) swapping sex stories and spilling every unshared moment we've had over the last few weeks.

Finally, Lou clears her throat and steers us back to the matter at hand, "So, what were you thinking outfit-wise?"

"Don't worry, I've got that one covered."

Lou's eyes widen with alarm, "Tell me it's not a leather pantsuit."

"To be fair, we looked hot as hell in those."

"True but I nearly killed myself trying to put it on."

I laugh, waving away her concern, "I promise it won't be as elaborate as matching pantsuits."

Lou raises a disbelieving eyebrow.

"Hon, you are just going to have to trust me on this one. Have I ever let you down?"

She opens her mouth then closes it.

I pretend to shoot her with an imaginary gun, "Exactly. I've got you and that is all you need to know. Your job is going to be finding cool designs for us to paint on each other."

"I think I can handle that." Lou tilts her head in thought, her golden-brown waves falling loosely over her shoulder.

"Do you think anyone else will be wearing paint?"

I grin, "If Nico has anything to do with it, absolutely."

We shuffle from the living room to my bedroom. The picture frame Lou gave me before the break hanging proudly above my desk. I catch her smile when she sees it, but before I can thank her for the thoughtful gift, my phone buzzes on my desk.

CODY: Not sure why the space next to me is so cold...

I grin, reaching over to grab my phone.

ME: We've been apart two hours. Johnson would say this adds to your whip tally.

CODY: Don't remind me. Your family is ruthless.

CODY: ... in a good way!

I laugh at the obvious backpedal while Lou busies herself with my open closet, flipping through the one section I didn't bring home.

ME: Good catch there, Captain.

CODY: I do my best. So, am I coming to you or are you coming to me tonight?

I glance at the pathetic mattress pad this university calls a bed. There is a four-inch-thick topper separating me from the terrible blue Styrofoam, but it is nowhere near restful material.

ME: Yours.

CODY: Sounds good. See you soon.

"Hey, why are all these clothes in my size?" Lou pulls out an adorable silver camisole that I have been saving for a special occasion.

"Are they?" I try for an innocent look but come up short.

"Stella, have you been buying clothes for me all year?" She gasps, bringing a hand to cover her mouth, "Is this where all our event outfits come from?"

She looks at my unopened suitcase on the floor and I quickly hold up my hands in surrender, "Okay, you got me. All those clothes hanging in there are for you. I didn't want to overwhelm you with them all at once, so that's why I save them for the perfect occasion."

Lou shakes her head, "This must have been so expensive. How much do I owe you?"

"Nothing. I bought these of my own free will."

"But Stella..."

I halt her words with a raised hand, "Just hear me out. There is one other thing I haven't told you about my family. My father is... well, extremely wealthy."

Lou blinks, "You're rich?"

I sigh and gesture towards my bed, "You might want to sit down for this one. To put it in perspective, let me tell you about the facilities in my family house..."

Chapter 23

♥

Cody

It's the first party I am attending with Stella as my girlfriend, so naturally she decided it would be best if I showed up alone.

For the most part, anyways.

"I feel like I should close my eyes for the grand reveal, what do you think?" Wes snaps his fingers before I can get a word in. "Actually, blindfolds might work better. That way I can't cheat."

I stifle a laugh, "Is the pitch-black room not enough for you?"

Wes sighs as if I just suggested we cancel the party and all go home early.

"Dude. The room can't be pitch black if people are glowing inside." He gestures towards the paint glowing from our naked torsos.

That's right. Stella managed to convince the entire lacrosse team to go shirtless. Not that it took much convincing with Nico and Wes already on board. The rest of the team has no choice but to follow.

I look at the green and purple swirls covering Wes' chest and abdomen, each one strategically placed so the glow makes him look more defined than usual. I, on the other hand, have the artistic ability of a two-year-old, so the blue streaks covering my chest are randomly placed on every spot I could reach.

"You make a fair point. I still don't think the blindfolds are necessary, though."

"Did someone say blindfolds? I'm in." Nico emerges from the dance floor, his brow glistening with sweat and orange warrior glow paint.

Wes groans, "I'm still recovering from walking in on you and a blindfolded Mark Chu. Worst roommate moment ever."

Nico laughs, his white teeth glowing brightly in the dark room, "I forgot about Chu! Man, that was a fun night. Shame he didn't want a repeat."

"Even if he did, you wouldn't have taken him back." Wes puts his hands together in prayer, "Nico Montez does not do repeats. Amen."

"Amen." Nico raises his glass and gives me a solemn nod. I shake my head at the duo, their status of childhood best friends shining through every interaction.

Glancing around the room, I admire the neon-themed decorations lighting up every corner. Nico and Wes somehow managed to convince Taber's one and only nightclub, BA$$, to host the event in exchange for a five dollar entry fee and a cash-only bar.

The local hotspot is nothing if not profitable.

Nico lets out a wolf whistle just as the song switches to a seductive Spanish beat, "Mi amigos, I think your ladies have arrived."

The change in tempo seems to change the atmosphere of the room. Or maybe it's just my heart rate that's changed.

Two figures move easily through the swarming crowd, the glow of Stella's hair making it easy to spot them. Wes looks like he's about two seconds from dropping to one knee, and if I'm being honest, I might not be far behind him.

"Trip, you look amazing. My balls feel blue already."

Nico cracks up while Lou rolls her eyes. The dark room makes it hard to tell if she is blushing, but based on previous interactions with her, I'd say chances are her cheeks are pretty red right now.

"Charming, Wes."

He grins, taking Lou's hand and pulling her flush against him. Neon green lines glow down Lou's back, dancing and intertwining with the crisscrossing straps of her white top.

It has Stella written all over it.

Wes shrugs modestly, "It's not my fault my girlfriend is a smoke show."

Lou rolls her eyes again, but I couldn't tell you what her reply is because suddenly my attention is trapped by the gorgeous girl standing in front of me.

My girl.

"Cat got your tongue, Captain?" Stella cocks out a hip, simultaneously capturing my attention and my libido all in one move.

"Wow." It's the best I can come up with as my eyes rake over her outfit, my balls tightening as they flick over the small but firm curves on display. My gaze comes to a stop at the pink paint trailing along her exposed torso.

She's wearing a crop top.

The darkness of the room keeps her scar hidden, but the significance of this moment hits me immediately. It's the first time I have ever seen Stella wear anything cropped, and tonight she chose to wear this lacy black number for all to see.

Pride bursts in my chest as I tug her closer and lean down to whisper in her ear, "Stel, I am so proud of you."

Stella gives me a small smile, silently asking for the reassurance she would never ask for out loud. Wrapping my fingers around her own, I quickly give them a squeeze, "I am all yours, tonight. Whenever and wherever you need me."

"Thank you."

Our moment comes to a screeching halt when Nico's favourite song comes on.

"OH MY GOD, I LOVE THIS SONG!" His scream draws our attention and next thing I know, Stella is grabbed by the hand and dragged towards the dance floor. My date mouths *sorry* as she heads off with my homosexual teammate, leaving me confused as to whether or not I should be offended.

"Cap, you gotta get her back. If you let Nico grind all over Stella, she'll fall in love by the end of the song." Wes gives me wide eyes, his arms still locked around Lou.

"Very funny."

"Nah man, I am serious. Nico is universally loved but choses to love very few." His lines sound like something straight out of a trashy tv show, but it does the trick. Ass in gear, I head for the gyrating mass on the dance floor.

Body odour hits me the second I merge with the crowd, the pulsing energy of the music feeding the energy on the dance floor. Two-stepping aside, I have never been the biggest fan of dancing, especially not at a club when half the people are too drunk to even dance and just stumble into one another.

I find Nico and Stella off to the side, safely tucked in the corner closest to the tables surrounding the bar. Breathing a sigh of relief, I note the absence of any grinding.

Stella laughs as Nico twirls her around, both of their bodies moving perfectly in synch to the beat. I watch, mesmerized by the fluidity of Stella's hips as she swings them around and around, her equally impressive abs flexing with each motion.

"Your girl sure can move." Wes materializes beside me with Lou tucked under one arm. She nods in agreement, "It's like watching a Shakira music video."

Wes grins, breaking his hold on Lou to sweep into a low bow, "Milady, would you be so kind as to accept this dance?"

She curtsies on cue, making me think this scene has played out more than once for this couple.

"Very gladly, kind sir." Lou takes his hand and I follow them to where Nico and Stella are tearing up the dance floor.

Stella

Everything is better when you're dancing.

That is the one and only lesson my mother ever taught me.

"GET IT GURL!" Nico claps as I drop it to the floor, my hips slowly grinding their way up and down an invisible pole. This probably isn't the type of dancing my mom pictured when she taught my brother and me the magic of rhythm, but I know she would applaud the effort.

Wes and Lou appear beside me, the two of them looking achingly cute in the blacklight glow of the nightclub. Lou is not what you would call a good dancer, but Wes takes the lead and wraps her arms around his neck, gently swaying her to the beat.

Looking around for my actual date, I'm about to go hunt him down when I feel someone come up behind me.

"I like watching you dance." Cody murmurs the words in my ear, his gravelly voice sending a jolt of heat to my core. Reaching behind me, I grab his hands and pull them to the front of my waist, enjoying the way his hard body fits perfectly against mine.

"I'll dance for you anytime you want." I change the tempo to a slower rhythm, pushing back against him just enough to make things interesting.

Cody's grip on my waist tightens as his movements shift to match mine. He skims his lips down my neck, planting a kiss on my collarbone before coming back up.

"Is that a promise?"

Goosebumps raise along my flesh despite the stifling heat of the room, my nipples already aching to be touched.

"Perform well tonight, Captain and you'll see for yourself."

I can't see Cody from our current position, but I feel the change in his body. His fingers burn through my jeans as he brings us closer, our movements going from semi-graceful gliding to hard core grinding.

Yup, we are that couple.

"GET A ROOM!" Nico pretends to cover his eyes while Wes laughs, his own dancing getting more inappropriate by the song. I try to catch Lou's eye to see how she is doing, but she's too preoccupied by the rookie doing his own *Magic Mike* rendition to notice.

The next song brings on a slower beat, so I turn around to enjoy the view from the front. Haphazard blue streaks line Cody's body from neck to waist, the glowing paint doing nothing to hide the thick muscles underneath. I run my hands up his chest, smearing blue in every direction.

Cody's eyes darken as his own hands start to wander, his fingers burning a trail over every inch of my skin.

"Would it be rude to leave soon?" My breathing hitches as Cody's fingers gently trace the uneven edges of my scar.

He smirks, "Is there someplace you'd rather be?"

I grin, rubbing myself shamelessly against the front of his jeans, "I'd rather be someplace private so you can be inside me."

A low growl escapes his throat, his normal brown eyes shining like a pair of obsidians.

"Let's go." He takes my hand before taking a step back, intertwining our fingers so we won't get separated in the crowd.

"Wait. Let me say bye to Lou first." Somewhere in our grinding session, we got separated from the others. Standing on my tip toes to look around, I spy Nico dancing atop the bar with a newfound dancing partner, but Wes and Lou are nowhere to be seen.

"Give me a second to text her and then we can go."

Cody nods and follows me to one of the booths lining the far back wall. I go to sit down when a pair of legs catches my attention.

"Is that..." Cody trails off as he looks at me with wide eyes.

I bite my lip to keep from laughing, "It sure is. Hey, Lou!"

The sexy black skinny jeans I bought for my roommate disappear into the booth before Lou's sheepish smile peeks around the corner.

"Oh, hey Stella. Sorry we disappeared like that." Blotches of green and purple paint cover her face and I can't hold back a laugh when Wes pops up looking equally rumpled beside her.

"Hey, Cap! Y'all heading home for the night?"

Cody coughs awkwardly into his hand, "Uh yeah. Do you guys want a ride home?"

"Nah, we're good. Trip and I are going to hang around for a bit longer, make sure Nico doesn't get into any trouble." Wes grins, giving us the full force of his dimples, "Text when you get home, okay?"

"Will do." We give them one last wave, and just like that, the couple picks up where they left off.

Our hands stay clasped together as Cody and I reach the exit door, making a mad dash for my black jeep parked across the street. Snow crunches under our feet as the bitter wind cuts straight through the thin material of my top and all but decimates Cody's bare chest.

I crank the heat the second we scramble inside, my automatic starting system making the leather seats slightly less cold than they would have been two minutes ago.

"Fuck, that was worse than your pool" Cody shivers against the leather seats, the blue tinge of his skin blending in with the dried paint.

I laugh, reaching over to angle the vents toward him, "I think Wes and Lou figured out the trick to stay warm. Body heat."

"Mm, I've never understood that."

I shift in my seat to look at him, "What? Fooling around in public?"

He nods, "Some things are better done at home."

"I mean, don't knock it till you try it. Unless you're scared of people seeing you naked?" I smirk, "Hate to be the one to break it to you, but Nico has probably checked you out in the changeroom. Wes too, for that matter."

Cody rolls his eyes, "Very funny. It's not about the public indecency."

"Oh?"

Cody leans back against his seat, the fire in his eyes doing wonders for my frozen lady bits.

"When we get naked, I want to *see* you naked. I want you spread out beneath me so I can take my time discovering every one of your hidden fantasies." He licks his lips and I feel it right between my legs.

"Guess I'd rather let the anticipation build so I can eat you properly, like a main course, rather than scarf down an appetizer somewhere convenient."

I blink, suddenly feeling the need to wind down a window.

Cody shrugs, "Anyways, that's just my opinion on the subject. Are we ready to go now?"

I stare at him, making no move to put the car in drive.

"What?" He feigns innocence, knowing damn well the visuals stuck in my head right now could classify me as a distracted driver.

"You did that on purpose."

"Did what?"

I narrow my eyes, "You know what."

Cody chuckles, leaning over to plant a kiss on my cheek.

"Hurry up and get us home. I'm getting hungry."

Chapter 24

♥

Cody

Stella attacks me the second we step through the door.

Her lean body latches onto mine, her strong legs wrapping tightly around my waist as we go stumbling through my dark living room. She starts kissing my neck as I flick on the lights, her tongue and breathless whispers making it difficult to ignore the growing bulge in my jeans.

I set Stella down on the kitchen counter and her cries of protest make me laugh.

"Don't tell me you are actually hungry."

I give nothing away as I take a step back and open the drawer below. She groans, laying back on my counter and making her shirt ride up in the process.

"You just ruined your own metaphor."

I grin, turning on the tap beside her and running a cloth beneath the hot water.

"Did you like being called my main course?"

She huffs, coming up to sit on her elbows, "I did before we made this little detour. You had me wet and ready."

I rinse out the cloth before bringing it to her stomach, "You should have more faith in me, O'Brien. Have I ever let you down before?"

She watches me closely as I rub the paint residue from her skin. My trek is slow but sure, carefully wiping away neon streaks with the precision of a surgeon. Her back arches as my meticulous cleaning goes further north, the angry juts of her nipples screaming at me from beneath black material.

Hooking a finger under the flimsy top, I tug it up and over her head, leaving Stella sitting half-naked on my kitchen counter.

It's a sight I could get used to.

"Do I get to rub you down now?" Big blue eyes beckon me closer, almost distracting me from the mission at hand.

"Nope." Tossing the cloth back into the sink, I pick Stella back up and carry her to the dinner table nearby.

Platinum hair splays out beneath her as I lay Stella flat on her back, the surprise on her face putting a smile on mine.

"So, no bed then?"

I grin, "I told you. I like to eat my food properly."

She moans, lifting her hips to help me pull the skin-tight jeans off her. Her bright pink underwear goes next, and I don't give her a second to think before I drop down and drag my tongue along her clit.

"Oh my god. You finally found it!" Her laughter turns into gasps as I push two fingers inside of her, sucking her bud between my lips as her slick folds welcome me.

"Yes! Right there, Cody." Her fingers fist my hair, urging me on.

I obey, following her commands and pushing her to the point of release just before backing off and starting the process all over. Stella writhes on the table, her body bucking in protest when I do it for a second time.

"Stop being an asshole." She grits her teeth, the grip on my hair tightening to the point of pain. I would be lying if I said I didn't enjoy it.

I tsk, "Let me finish my meal in peace."

"You are going to regret this five minutes from now."

"Five more minutes? I think I can handle that."

Stella levels me with a glare, and I respond by slipping my tongue inside her. She jerks as my fingers follow suit, and soon I give her the happy ending she's looking for.

I wipe my mouth with a grin, watching Stella come back down from her orgasm. I've lived in this house for two years now, and I don't think this table has ever been put to better use.

Stella

"Is this why you don't drink alcohol?"

Cody traces my tattoo with a lazy finger, the bolded letters screaming out from my otherwise pale complexion. We're lying on top of his comforter, naked except for each other's company. After the dinner table episode, Cody and I finally made it to bed.

And as Donna would say dot, dot, dot.

"Yes." I swallow, "If it weren't for an impaired driver, my mother would still be alive."

Cody's eyes soften, "That doesn't mean you need to punish yourself."

"I don't consider not drinking a punishment." My words come out sharper than I intended but I can't help it. Cody is poking a wound that never healed properly, triggering all my defense mechanisms.

"You know that's not what I meant." The finger tracing my tattoo veers off towards my spine, drawing indecipherable symbols along each vertebra.

I sigh, the tension leaving my body with each soothing touch, "I know, I'm sorry. It's just... It's a difficult subject for me."

"I understand that, but you shouldn't keep it bottled up inside." Cody pauses, chewing on his lip before continuing, "You aren't going to like what I have to say, but before you go on the offence, just think about it, okay?"

I nod, mentally bracing myself for impact.

"Have you ever thought about seeing someone? To talk about the accident and the panic attacks?"

I feel my hackles start to raise, a snarky comment forming on the tip of my tongue. But instead of letting it out, I exhale, remembering Cody's request.

To ask for help is to show weakness.

My father's voice rings through immediately, making me physically wince against Cody's pillows.

"I can't. It goes against everything my father taught me."

Cody watches me silently, his face pensive.

I try again, hoping for him to understand, "Mo and I were raised differently. We don't go around showing our pain to the world, it's a sign of weakness. I haven't seen my brother cry since he turned twelve and my father sat him down and explained the expectations of what it means to be a man." My throat tightens at the memory, the one and only time my mother and father ever fought in front of us.

"Just because he's a boy doesn't mean he can't have feelings, Jonathan." Mother stands with her hands on her hips, the angry swish of her dress matching the tension in the air.

Father shakes his head, "When I'm gone, Maurice is going to need to be the man of the house. He can't do that if he breaks under the slightest pressure."

Mother throws up her hands, "A man is allowed to break! Everyone breaks, it is only a matter of where and when. There is nothing shameful about a woman who cries, so why should it be shameful for a man to cry?"

Mo sniffs next to me, his tear-stained face puffy and red.

"Look at him! No one will ever take him seriously like that." Father whirls around, the look in his eyes making it clear there will be no more arguing.

"Maurice, get yourself cleaned up. I don't ever want to see your cheeks damp again, do you understand?"

Mo turns and scurries down the hall as mother shakes her head sadly, "Don't raise our children how you were raised, Jonathan. Times are different, and now more than ever children need support not judgement from their parents."

For a fleeting moment, father looks guilty, "I don't know any different." He sighs, running a hand down his tired face, "I'm trying my best here."

Mother rushes over to him, "I know you are. But you can't be so cold with the children. One day I might not be around, and it's going to be up to you to give them the love and support they need in this world."

I back away, turning to run after Mo as father pulls mother close.

"Don't go and we won't have that problem."

Cody clears his throat, bringing me back to the present.

"Did you do physiotherapy after the accident?"

I frown, confused as to where this is going, "Of course."

"So, when your body needs help recovering, you provide for it, but when it comes to your mind, you just ignore it?"

I open my mouth then close it. Because as much as I hate to admit it, Cody has a valid point.

"I've never thought about it like that."

He gives me a crooked smile, "It's just something to consider. Not that I don't love our morning panic attacks together, but it would be nice to see you wake up rested for once."

I laugh softly, "Pretty sure I owe you about a month's worth of sleep at this point."

Cody chuckles, leaning in to press a kiss against my forehead.

"I'll send you an invoice by the end of the year."

We crawl under the covers together, limbs tangling together in a warm cocoon I never want to leave. Just as Cody's breathing grows deeper, I reach over and grab my phone, setting my usual alarm for the next morning. Hesitating, I open my reminders and set a new one to look for trauma therapists near Taber University.

Cody is right, I do need help. The fact I have yet to wake up to this alarm in over two years is reason enough to at least look into my options.

Chapter 25

♥

Cody

I snatch the ball away from Hunter, pivot, and hurl it back across the gym.

Hunter gives me a dirty look before running to join the back of the line. I've had the team doing drills for the last hour, trying to get as much technical training as possible before tournament season kicks off again.

"Cap, you've got to let some of the guys make it past the defense line. I'm falling asleep over here."

I turn to see our goaltender lounging on the ground, using his lacrosse stick as an uncomfortable pillow. Nico's helmet is pushed onto his forehead, and unlike the rest of the team, there isn't a drop of perspiration on it.

"The man's got a new boo, he's feeling lucky." Mason gives me a shit-eating grin from his position on the defense line. The rest of the team is lined up near the massive tiger mural on the wall, Taber's mascot growling at every player who has tried and failed to take a shot on net today.

"More like he's been getting lucky." Nico says the unhelpful comment loud enough for the rest of the rookies to hear, drawing hoots and cheers from the lineup.

I ignore them and wave for the next person to go. Wes charges forward, his speed considerably faster than it was at the start of the year, and almost manages to make it past me with a quick deke to the right. I catch the swerve just in time, knocking him off-balance with a shoulder check before stealing the ball and passing it to Mason. Wes grunts and returns to the line while Nico makes a show of yawning behind me.

"Can I check out early? I've got a hot date to get ready for tonight."

I glance at the clock on the wall, "What time is your date?"

"Nine-thirty. But prep starts at six." Nico shoots me a wink, "Not all of us can roll out of bed looking sexy as hell."

Mason glances at the rookie, "I don't know man, you always look good to me."

"Aw babe, you're making me blush."

I pointedly look at the clock again, "Your prep time is three hours away."

"That gives me just enough time to finish visualizing. Got to be in the right mindset to score some goals if ya know what I mean."

I shake my head, wishing I could cut practice short so I could have my own hot date. It's been three days since I last saw Stella, and every minute we've been apart is a minute she's been weighing on my mind.

"If I'm stuck here, so are you. Next!"

STELLA: My first appointment is Friday 4PM. Think I could swing by your place after?

ME: Of course, but I don't want you to drive.

My phone rings the second I hit send, and I grin as Stella's aggravated voice comes down the line.

"Don't be ridiculous, I am fully capable of driving myself to therapy."

"It's not about being capable, Stel. It's going to be an emotional experience for you, and I don't want you to be at risk because you're distracted."

Stella goes silent and I can hear the counter arguments forming in her head.

Finally, she sighs, "Fine. Can you drop me off and pick me up then?"

I smile, "Don't sound so disappointed. At least we'll get to see each other." Quickening my pace to a jog, I run through the empty corridors of the university, my night class having started five minutes ago.

"Yeah." Stella exhales through the phone, "I miss you."

The pang in my chest feels dangerously close to homesickness that's associated with a person.

"I miss you too. I knew not seeing you was going to be difficult but..."

"It's difficult." She laughs, finishing my sentence and just the sound of it makes my day seem a whole lot brighter.

"And it's only been three days. Imagine what tournament season is going to be like."

I hate being the one to voice concern, but it's a concern that has been bothering me for a while now. It has only been 72 hours since I woke up beside Stella and gave her a goodbye kiss, but that feels like an eternity ago. We live in the same city and yet our schedules make it feel like we're two boats passing in the night. Even our gym routine from first semester has been thrown off with additional lacrosse practices.

"Times three."

"Huh?"

Stella laughs, a small sound that lacks any sense of humour, "We're going to have to do this for the next three years. Until you run out of eligibility to play lacrosse. And by then, we should both be graduated."

I frown, pausing outside my classroom door. The lecture is already underway, but this conversation is more important.

"Don't do that."

"Do what?"

"Make it sound like we're not worth it."

Stella sighs, "It's just a lot to think about."

Leaning against the nearby wall, I exhale, wishing the answers were closer than they are right now.

"You know, a girl once told me you can't look at relationships with a rational point of view. We're always going to be too busy or too complicated unless you're willing to fight for it."

"She sounds like a smart one, that girl." I can hear the smile in Stella's voice.

"She's brilliant. And sexy as hell."

"Oh? Please, go on."

I chuckle, "There aren't enough words in this world to describe you, Stel. You are wonderful. You are kind. You are mine."

"And now he rhymes." Stella laughs, "I love you, Ellsworth."

"I love you too, O'Brien."

The words come out as easy as breathing, a truth that has always been known but just now spoken out loud.

Stella sighs, "I should let you get to class. Text me later, okay?"

"Always." I clear my throat before continuing, "And hey, we're going to figure this out. It's stressing me as well, but as long as we stay strong and stay together, it's all going to work out."

"I believe you. Now, run along before you get detention."

I laugh and hang up the phone, pushing through the door and snagging an open seat at the back. The professor gives me a nod of acknowledgement, but no one else spares me a second glance.

There's only one grinning fool in the back who realizes at least one person in this room is completely and madly in love.

Stella

Lou takes pity on me the next morning.

"Okay, I'll workout with you." My sullen mood skyrockets, the beaming smile spreading across my face making her own scrunch up in a grimace.

"But," Lou holds up a hand, "No burpees. Or anything else that might make me puke."

"Deal." We shake on it, and I practically skip all the way back to our dorm to get ready. I've been in a bit of a funk not seeing Cody all week, but I've been doing my best not to let it show.

Obviously my efforts didn't pay off.

"I don't have to change, do I?" Lou tugs self-consciously at the oversized concert t-shirt tucked into her mom jeans. The fact she was thinking of wearing jeans to the gym tells you everything there is to know about Lou's exercise regime.

"I'm choosing not to answer that. Here, I've got you covered." I dash to my closet and return with an adorable gym outfit in my hands.

Lou takes the offering with a frown, "Why would you buy workout gear for me? You know I've never stepped foot in Taber's gym."

I shrug, "I always knew one day I'd convince you to join me. My willpower is just too strong."

She mumbles something under her breath as she takes the matching tank top and leggings, the crease between her brows prominent as she studies the fabric.

"Are you sure this is my size? It looks too small."

I call over my shoulder as I head into my room to change, "Have I ever steered you wrong when it comes to outfits?"

"It's probably best if I don't answer that."

"Put an end to this misery." Lou flops to the ground, her baby blue tank top looking spectacular against the backdrop of the core mat.

"You haven't done a sit up yet."

"Sit up? Since when are we doing sit ups? I thought we were done the workout." It takes every ounce of willpower not to laugh at Lou's baffled expression.

"Hon, we just finished warm up."

Lou gasps, "But we were running!"

I nod my head patiently, "You have to warm up your body before starting the hard stuff. We were only on the treadmill for ten minutes."

Lou scowls and I decide not to point out that she walked for nine of those ten minutes.

"What are we doing now then?"

"Well, normally I pick different HIIT exercises to rotate through, but I thought we'd start with some easier bodyweight exercises."

Lou gives me a blank stare and I sigh, "Let's try doing a few sit ups and see how they go. Try for five."

She starts with painful slowness, her knees knocking together each time she makes it to the top. My cheering goes a long way to put back the smile on Lou's face, and by the time she finishes five sit ups, she almost looks like she is having a good time.

Lou beams, "Are we done now?"

So maybe not that much of good a time.

I shake my head, "You've got two more rounds and then we are going to do some dumbbells." The smile slips from her face and the scowl makes a grand return.

"Do you want to know the fun part about dumbbells?" I motion for her to lean in, which she does, but not before giving me the evil eye.

"We can use the mirrors to check out the gym bros."

Lou looks at me quizzically, "I thought you and Cody were a thing now?"

I wave my hands impatiently, "It's not about the guys themselves, it's about admiring physique. Cody would appreciate my appreciation."

Lou gives me a disbelieving look, so I play my final card.

"The best part is watching grown men pose to themselves in the mirror. Even the unfit ones do it, it's like a free-for-all vanity contest around here."

"You're kidding."

"I am dead serious. Take a look for yourself."

Lou scrambles to stand beside me, and I nod over to the weight section across from us.

"Blonde in the left corner. Red shirt, black shorts. Looks like a swimmer with those lats."

We watch in anticipation as the Dorito-shaped man finishes his hammer curls, drops the weights to the floor, and casually turns to the side, watching his arms pop with the infamous Mr. Universe pose.

"Does he not know everyone can see him?" Lou starts to giggle as he drops the pose and resumes lifting like nothing ever happened.

I shrug, "I have no idea, but they all do it. Gym bros are a different breed." Nudging Lou's shoulder, I call out our next contender, "Pornstar moustache, 12 o'clock. Checking his teeth for lunchtime leftovers."

Lou gasps, "He just pulled something out of his teeth and ate it."

"Nothing like a protein boost mid-lift."

We crack up, drawing attention from other gym patrons nearby. The late morning crowd isn't as intense as the early-morning one, so I'm not too concerned about ruining the do-or-die atmosphere.

Lou's still laughing as she wipes tears from her eyes, "Have you ever caught Cody doing something like that? He's technically a gym bro, isn't he?"

"Oh, for sure. You know the way he runs his hand through his hair?" I mimic the motion, making sure to pause at the top to flex my bicep.

"It's a good move."

"I've caught him practicing it in a mirror at home."

Lou grins, "No way."

"Yes way. The only reason I didn't give him shit about it is because it's one of my favourite moves." I wink, "Outside the bedroom, of course."

Lou's cheeks flush pink just as a familiar voice reaches me.

"O'Brien! Hitting the gym before and after the sun comes up now, eh?" Unruly dark curls pop into my peripheral and I turn to my friend with a smile.

"Any excuse to see you, Stephen."

He sighs, placing a hand above his heart, "Always knew you would come around. The 'fro grows on you, doesn't it?"

Lou laughs, drawing Stephen's attention. His dark eyes sparkle as they take in my gorgeous roommate.

"And who might this be? Cody is going to be pissed he was so easily replaced."

"This is Lou, my roommate. She's dating Wes from the-

"Lacrosse team! Hell, I love that guy. The team gets to train in the high-performance gym, away from us mere mortals, but he always makes sure to stop by and say hi."

Lou smiles, "That sounds like Wes."

"Small world." Stephen shakes his head, a huge grin taking over his face, "Taber University just keeps getting better and better."

I laugh, "You've been here too long."

"Maybe." A thoughtful gleam brightens his eyes, "Where has Cody been recently? I haven't seen him since before the break."

Lou shoots me a concerned look, no doubt worried her gym efforts to cheer me up have been in vain. Pushing down the sudden heartache, I paste a smile onto my face.

"Tournament season is fast approaching. Practices are mornings and afternoons now."

What I don't mention are the extra classes Cody is having to take due to his injury first semester. Our mornings and evenings have been stolen right out from under us, and once tournaments start up, our weekends will be gone as well. Cody keeps talking about spending our nights together, but when he has to get up at 5AM every morning and doesn't get home until 10PM, the last thing I want to do is take away those few precious hours of sleep.

We went from spending every waking hour together to scheduling hangout times once, sometimes twice a week if we're lucky.

The whiplash hurts to say the least.

"Bummer. Do you two still find time to bicker?"

Lou laughs, reclaiming Stephen's full attention.

"I am glad someone else noticed their constant arguing!"

I cross my arms with a huff, "We are just two opinionated people. Sometimes we bump heads."

"Sometimes?" Stephen grins, turning to Lou, "You should have seen them first semester. Every morning it was like watching two lions fight over a gazelle. Pure entertainment."

Lou smirks, "Who would win?"

I narrow my eyes, "Choose your next words wisely."

He chuckles, "With one exception, I always place my bets on O'Brien. And to-date, I have never lost a bet."

I nod, satisfied with his answer while Lou raises her eyebrow in question.

"What was the one exception?"

Stephen grins, "Who was going to end up with O'Brien."

I blink in surprise, "There was a bet for that?"

"Of course. And for that one, my money was always on Cody."

Chapter 26

♥

Friday, 3:30 PM.

Cody

MASON: Get your ass to the gym, the USport representative will be here any minute.

Resisting the urge to smash my phone against a nearby wall, I pinch the bridge of my nose and pull up Stella's number. It rings through and I suck down a breath before I lose my shit.

Why did the USport representative have to choose today of all days to make an appearance? Took them months to respond to the assistant coaching request I sent back in September.

I try Stella's number again but no answer. The time on my phone blinks at me mockingly, the numbers counting down the minutes until I was supposed to drive Stella to her first therapy session.

Fuck. Why isn't she answering her phone?

WES: Hey man, not sure what's going on but wanted to check and see if you were ok?? We kind of need you at the gym right now.

I clench my jaw, feeling my molars pop. This whole situation is bullshit. We only got notified about this mandatory meeting ten minutes ago, and as the team captain, there is no way I cannot attend.

Especially considering I was the one who sent the request in the first place.

ME: What is Lou's number? I can't get a hold of Stella.

WES: Here it is. Should I be worried?

Ignoring his last text, I hit Lou's number and breathe a sigh of relief when she answers on the first ring.

"Hey, it's Cody. Is Stella around?"

"Oh, hi Cody. Let me check." Movement echoes through the phone, the sound of a door opening and closing before Lou hops back on the line.

"No, sorry. I think she went for a run to blow off some steam before her appointment."

"She went for a run without her phone?" I exhale, willing myself to get a reign on my emotional spiral. My frustration and now concern for Stella's safety puts me about two seconds from blowing my top.

"Never mind, I'll discuss that with her later. Right now, I need your help."

"Me?" The surprise in her voice has me softening my tone.

"Yes. Has Stella talked to you about this upcoming appointment?"

Shuffling breaks through the background and I picture Lou pacing the small space of her and Stella's dorm.

"A little bit. She's going to talk to someone about the accident that took her mother."

A hint of relief hits me knowing that Lou is in the loop.

"Right. It's going to be a rollercoaster of emotions for her today, so I was supposed to be her ride but the USport representative just showed up."

As if on cue, my phone starts buzzing with team chat messages asking about my whereabouts. Now is not the time to be MIA.

"Oh, that's no problem. You just need me to drop her off?

I exhale, "Please. If it were anyone but USport, I would blow them off."

"I understand. And Stella will too. As captain, your team has to come first."

I frown at Lou's words, my stomach churning uneasily with the matter-of-fact way she said them. As if it's perfectly normal for me to put a team meeting above the needs of my girlfriend.

How fucked up is that?

Lou pauses, as if sensing my rising distress, "I will let you know if anything happens. And if the team meeting runs long, just shoot me a text and I can pick her up as well."

The grip on my phone loosens slightly, "Thank you, Lou."

I take a second to collect myself as the frustrations of my relentless schedule and guilt of bailing on Stella threatens to overwhelm me.

The worst part about it all is that it's my choice. I am the one who chose to take on the responsibility of being a varsity athlete, and I am the one who has yet to learn how to delegate. The meeting today was supposed to be a step in the right direction, a step towards facilitating the captain's role as team leader, coach, and event planner.

But now, I'm not so sure I want the role of captain anymore.

Marching with the fury of Silverwood's infamous lacrosse bully, I make my way towards the gymnasium where a stranger is going to tell me whether or not Taber got approved for the funding to bring on an assistant coach for next year's season. It's the epitome of my career as Taber's lacrosse captain, but instead of thinking about the Tigers next season, I find myself wishing I could be driving my girlfriend to therapy.

Stella

I hate feeling vulnerable.

Okay, fine. I'm sure nobody enjoys being vulnerable, but for me it's a whole different level. It's a matter of ego, of course, but it's also a matter of self-preservation.

Up until Cody Ellsworth, I had no trouble burying my insecurities from the world. Until that blonde fauxhawk marched into my life and dug up all those messy emotions, I was buzzing like a bee without a care in the world.

Am I still grieving my dead mother after two years? For sure.

Do I have a PTSD episode every morning? Sure, but I don't mind waking up early.

To keep things neat and tidy, we have to compartmentalize. And sometimes that means pushing aside minor inconveniences that don't always leave me feeling great. But according to Cody, that is me avoiding my problems.

He's got a point, but it's not completely accurate. You can't avoid something if you simple choose not to address it.

Right?

"Do you want me to go in with you?" Lou squints out the windshield, assessing the nondescript white building in front of us. We've been parked outside my new therapist's building for ten minutes now and I have yet to make a move to leave the car.

I shake my head, "Thank you, but I should probably do this alone. Just give me another minute."

"It feels weird being in enemy territory, hey?"

I nod, glancing around Silverwood's small downtown area. Taber's biggest rival also happens to be the only town within a 100km radius that has an on-call therapist, so Lou and I had to venture across hostile borders so I can spill my deepest, darkest secrets to a stranger.

Can't wait.

Lou smiles, pointing to a store down the road, "Lacey would love that garden shop. I'll have to keep it in mind as an activity we could do next year."

Following her finger, I spy the greenhouse doubling as a boutique next to an equally adorable coffee shop. Rival status aside, Silverwood has the kind of charm that makes you want to spend your days walking downtown and getting lost in the mom-and-pop shops you only find in towns this small.

If I wasn't a loyal Tiger, I would be seriously tempted to spend more time here.

"That's a great idea." I take a deep breath and finally unbuckle my seatbelt, "Okay, I am going in now."

"You got this!" Lou gives me a reassuring smile as I make a move to open the door. Just before pulling the handle, I pause and glance back at her.

"Do you think you could wait ten minutes before leaving? Just in case this doesn't work out and I come running out screaming."

Lou nods, "Of course. I wasn't planning on leaving until I was sure you weren't going to make a break for it."

"Thank you." Before I can give it any more thought, I yank on the handle and hurl myself from the car. Forcing myself to keep walking all the way to the door, I knock before the doubt has a chance to creep in.

The door swings open and white-blonde hair assaults my vision. I blink as a guy my age comes to a halt upon seeing me, the shock crossing his face a mirror image to the one crossing my own.

"Stella O'Brien." He gives me a cool nod, locking me in a penetrating gaze.

"Skylar Vin." Otherwise known as the younger brother of the psychopath who injured Cody last semester. The lacrosse bully that is Vector Vin.

Skylar shifts, drawing my attention to the massive sketchbook tucked under one arm. I consider making a crack about trauma being artistic inspiration but decide to keep my mouth shut. Even though we've been attending the same lacrosse games for years, Skylar and I have never hit it off.

To be honest, something about *him* seems a bit off, but then again, it could just be the bad image Vector projects over them both.

"A little far from home, aren't you?" Besides the white-blonde hair, there aren't many similarities between the Vin brothers. Where Vector is all brawn and bulk, Skylar is lean and slender. And while Vector's nasally voice wouldn't win him any singing competitions, Skylar's smooth undertones gives him radio host potential.

I shrug, "It's always good to broaden one's horizons."

Not a trace of a smile is cracked by my response, Skylar simply goes back to studying me. I study him right back, refusing to be intimidated by his older brother's reputation. My gaze dances between his blue and brown irises, the opposing colours making each of them stand out in a strange but beautiful way.

"Stella?" A friendly looking woman peeks over Skylar's shoulder, her proximity making him hunch out of the way. With a wave, she gestures for me to come in, "Please, make yourself at home. Skylar was just leaving."

I give Skylar a tight smile as he ambles past me, but he ducks his head, avoiding my gaze and yanking up the hood of his Sabers sweater.

Weird.

Turning my attention back to the matter at hand, I tentatively step through the doorway as my new therapist chatters cheerfully, "My name is Karen, and I am here to help any way I can. What that will look like will be up to you."

She leads me through a small office, passing what looks to be her workstation, and heads towards a large sitting room. Karen gestures for me to take a seat on the beige couch lining the far wall while she makes herself comfortable on the chair directly across from me.

A vintage clock ticks on the wall, the insistent chiming keeping in time with the nervous tapping of my foot. I force myself to stop, wishing I had thought ahead to bring a water bottle or something to occupy my hands with.

The wooden table sitting between us catches my attention and I notice for the first time the bright yellow box of tissues sitting upon it.

Casually adjusting her floral dress, Karen nods towards them, "You've noticed our sunshine tissues. Each one has a different message written on it, something uplifting to help when these sessions get difficult." She smiles kindly at me, "All patients are welcome to help themselves. Sometimes these sessions can be overwhelming."

I try not to let my horror show as I contemplate reading a snot-covered pocket card in front of a stranger. I can't tell if that is better or worse than the simple act of crying.

"Thanks, but I can assure you those will not be necessary."

Karen nods thoughtfully, "Of course. They are there just in case." She grabs a pen from the cupholder beside her and clicks it, "Shall we get started then?"

"Sure."

Karen makes herself comfortable and gives me a warm smile, "Did you book this appointment, or did someone do it for you?"

"I did. At the encouragement of others."

"I see." She pauses to scribble some notes, "Tell me, Stella, what are you hopping to gain from these sessions?"

I force my gaze from the ancient clock and go back to bouncing my leg.

"Closure, I guess. I struggle with panic attacks."

"When did these panic attacks start?"

"After my mother died." My eyes start to burn, and I mentally curse.

"Here, dear, take a tissue. It will help, trust me."

I nod, reaching forward to grab a radiant tissue from the equally bright box. I unfold the note and crack a smile at the ridiculously cheerful message waiting for me.

You have already taken the first and hardest step!

Karen meets my gaze with kind eyes, "Are you ready to continue, Stella?"

I steal another glance at the clock. Fifty-five minutes to go.

"Maybe I'll be needing these tissues after all."

Karen chuckles, adding another note to her clipboard, "Everyone does."

Chapter 27

♥

Cody

The second Stella exits the building, I can tell something is wrong.

Quickly hopping out of my car, I close the distance between us and immediately pull her into a hug. She slumps against me, her arms hanging loose by her sides.

"Don't let go." She murmurs the words against my chest and the raw vulnerability in her voice just about breaks my heart.

"Wouldn't dream of it." I pull her closer, wishing my hold was strong enough to protect her from the outside world. Not because Stella can't fight her own battles, but because she deserves to be saved.

We stay like that for a long time, long enough for the next patient to roll up and enter the building. A few more minutes tick by until finally Stella pulls away with a heavy exhale, "Okay, we can go. Thanks for that."

"No need to thank me, Stel." I interlink our fingers and squeeze them gently as I guide her back to the car. Stella climbs in and we fall silent, her looking out the windshield while I look at her.

"How did it go?" It feels like a stupid question to ask given the redness around her eyes, but it's one that needs to be addressed.

"Terrible." She turns to me with a sigh, "But weirdly liberating. I've booked in to see her again next week."

"Do you think it helped?"

Stella shrugs, taking a long strand of hair and threading it through her fingers, "Hard to tell. Karen had a lot of productive things to say, she mentioned some coping mechanisms we can slowly implement into my lifestyle. It's going to take a lot of time and energy, but I do think it will help. Eventually."

"Sounds promising."

"It does. I just didn't expect it to be so... draining, I guess." Stella gives me a weak smile, "Who knew talking could be so strenuous?"

I chuckle, leaning over to plant a kiss on her forehead, "You did a lot more than talking today, Stel. You took the first step to recovery."

"Recovery fucking sucks."

I grin, turning the ignition and putting the car in drive, "It sure does."

Stella's spunk starts to return when we arrive at my house. We enter the kitchen and her eyes all but glow when they take in the elaborate spread I laid out on my kitchen countertop earlier today.

"Did you make all this?"

I nod, "Got my mom to send me some family recipes the other day. Figured I needed someone besides myself to judge my cooking skills."

"Ooh, are those spring rolls?" Grabbing one straight from the pan, Stella takes a bite and moans, "This is amazing, Cody. Thank you."

I grin, handing her a plate, "This might help."

"I am definitely coming back for seconds." Stella hums to herself as she loads up on the miscellaneous dishes I prepared the night before. Spring rolls, pasta salad, gazpacho soup, and dinner rolls all making the strange combination that is tonight's dinner.

We sit side-by-side at the dinner table, our knees casually brushing.

"I had no idea you could cook." Happily ripping a bun in half, Stella dips it into her soup with a smile, "You are hereby nominated as the chef in this relationship."

"So, I'm responsible for all our future meals together?"

"You got it, Captain."

I shake my head, "Saddling me with all the work. Typical."

Stella laughs, pushing away her empty bowl and turning to watch me finish my own. Her blue eyes seem darker than normal, her mischievous glint nowhere in sight. Leaning over, I grab the edge of her chair and pull it closer.

Stella laughs and hops from her chair to mine, making herself comfortable on my lap.

I sigh, finally feeling complete, "I missed you this week."

"I missed you too." Reaching up to cup my jaw, Stella leans in and plants a gentle kiss on my lips. She pulls away with a smile, "But now we get to make up for lost time."

My brows tug into a frown, "You've had a long day. Let's not push it."

"What are we pushing exactly?" Shifting so she's straddling me, Stella grinds against me, her teasing movements doing nothing to help my argument.

I clench my teeth, willing my shaft not to respond, "I don't want to take advantage of you."

"What if *I* want to take advantage of *you*?" Stella continues to grind against me, and despite my mental protests, my hands wander down to the firm cheeks of her ass.

"I am trying to be good, here, Stel. You're making this hard."

"Mm, that's not the only thing that's hard, now is it?" She grins, reaching down to stroke me through my sweatpants. And I let her because when it comes to this girl, I am defenseless.

Completely and utterly at her mercy.

"Hellion." Surrendering to the energy growing between us, I yank her in for a kiss. She gasps against my lips as the grip on her ass tightens, the tempo of her hips growing faster with every stroke of my tongue.

Stella pulls me off the chair and onto the floor, her hands making quick work of my shirt as she climbs on top of me. Her eyes glint dangerously as her nails rake down my chest, my hips jerking at the sensation.

"You know, this would be a lot more comfortable in be-

Stella steals my sentence with a kiss, making me groan as her hands dig into the waist band of my pants and tugs them off. Her mouth follows the trail her nails made, her tongue tracing every outline of muscle she can find. Before she can get to the jackpot, I yank her back up and strip her to a more equal point of undress.

I'm still laying on my back when I slip a finger inside her, the new position giving me a much better angle to appreciate the small but perfect tits bouncing above me. She moans when I slip a second finger in, my thumb rubbing lazy circles around her swollen bud.

I almost have her at a climax when she removes my hand and pins it above my head.

"Is this the part where you take advantage of me?"

Stella grins, "Told you I always wanted to save a horse." She moves further down, positioning her entrance at my tip before taking me in.

I groan as her body welcomes me home, "Should I go grab a cowboy hat?"

Stella starts to move, her breathy pants making my hips thrust up to meet hers.

"Wouldn't want to ruin your hair." We grin at each other, bodies and minds completely intertwined.

Stella lifts herself almost completely off me before slamming back down, repeating the process over and over again as we draw closer to the finish line. I grip her waist, helping her along as she takes us both on a ride, her movements smooth and precise as she pushes us right over the edge. I feel her climax right before my own, her inner walls clenching me tightly as we finally reach the desired release.

Platinum hair brushes my face as Stella smiles down at me, her flushed face and sparkling eyes easily making this moment the best part of my week.

Stella

"My back will never be the same."

I burst out laughing as I climb off Cody, my knees already bruising from the unforgiving hardwood. Cody groans as he sits up, and I crack up when I see the red indents lining his broad back.

"Don't worry, you'll bounce back."

"Animal." Cody grins at me, grabbing his sweatpants from the floor, "Not sure if the horse was saved but I sure got a ride."

I laugh, stealing his shirt and pulling it on, "Sounds like it worked in your favour."

"Sure did." The smile falls from Cody's face as he pulls something from his pocket, "Shit. We forgot to use a condom."

I wave away his concern, "I have an IUD. And I'm clean."

"Same." Cody runs a hand through his hair, his biceps popping admirably, "We can still use condoms on a regular basis, just because we didn't today doesn't have to mean anything."

I smile, touched by his thoughtfulness, "Feels a lot better raw, don't you think?"

"I mean, yeah, but I don't want you to feel pressured."

"Ellsworth, you couldn't pressure me into something if you tried."

Cody lets out an exasperated sigh, "Forget I said anything."

I smile, deciding to cut the poor man a break, "I appreciate the concern."

Falling into a comfortable silence, we clear the table and wash the dishes. This domestic part of our relationship feels so natural, so normal that it makes me wish we had more time for mundane moments like this.

"How did the meeting with USport go?" I ask the question as Cody passes me a clean plate to put away.

"It went better than I was expecting, actually." His forearms plunge back into the soapy water and I take the moment to enjoy the view. This man should never wear a shirt in my presence.

"Will the team be getting an assistant coach for next year?"

He frowns, "I think so. There was talk of bringing back a graduated student, but nothing is confirmed."

I tilt my head, "Isn't that a good thing?"

He sighs, "Yes, it is. Even if it's not a graduated student, chances are high that USport will fund an assistant coach for Taber."

"So, the problem is..."

"I don't know if I want to play lacrosse next year."

I nearly drop the plate in my hands. Out of all the scenarios running through my head for the next three years, Cody not being part of the lacrosse team was not one of them.

Pulling the drain at the bottom of the sink, Cody leans back against the counter and looks at me, "It's been a lot recently. Too much time and not enough results."

I carefully place the plate in its cabinet before turning to face him, "Is this about us?"

"Partly." Cody meets my stare before going on, "I'm burnt out, Stel. Getting my face bashed in last semester changed my perspective on priorities when it comes to lacrosse. Sooner or later, I'm going to take a hit and I might not be able to get back up again."

I can only stare as he continues, "And I don't want to see you once a week for the next three years. It's not fair to you, it's not fair to me, and it's certainly not fair to the development of our relationship."

"But won't you miss it? That's your team, Cody. Those are your players."

"They are my players, and they are my team, but you are my future." The raw look in his eyes is one I have never seen before.

"And that is more important than any team or tournament I could compete in." Cody shakes his head, his eyes glistening, "This last week was terrible. All I could think about was seeing you, and then when I couldn't be there for you today? I just about killed somebody."

My heart clenches, adrenalin and fear cursing through my bloodstream.

"I don't want you to give up something you love and then regret it down the road."

"Don't you get it? *You* are what I love. You are the only reason I ever want to wake up before 5AM every morning."

I choke out a laugh, "Karen should be helping with that soon."

Stepping towards me, Cody tucks a strand of hair behind my ear, "It doesn't matter if we're up at the crack of dawn every day for the rest of our lives. As long as we're together, I'm happy."

I lean into his touch, smiling against his hand, "It sounds like you've already made up your mind. Guess we'll be seeing a lot of each other next fall, huh?"

"Next fall?" An eyebrow goes up, "You aren't getting away from me that easily, O'Brien. I'm going to delegate some of my captain duties so I can ravish my girlfriend as much as possible."

I smirk, "Not sure your back can handle any more ravishing."

"Guess we'll have to take turns on who gets to be sore." Cody grins, grabbing my thighs and hauling me up against him. His shirt I'm wearing rides up in the process, making it obvious I'm already ready for him.

"Are we going to the bedroom this time?" I blink innocently as my legs wrap around his waist, ready to be carried to bed.

"Oh, no. There are a few more rooms you have yet to see." Cody grins and starts walking us towards the office next door.

Chapter 28

♥

Cody

I pull Wes and Nico aside after our morning practice on Monday.

"What's up, Cap?" Wes shakes his hair back and forth, sweat flying everywhere. The new cardio elements I've incorporated into our training has made Monday mornings public enemy number one.

Stella would be proud.

"Just wanted to have a quick discussion about next year." I pause, knowing this is the point of no return. "After this spring, I am stepping down from the team."

I wait for the wave of guilt or remorse to hit me, but it never does.

Wes blinks, "You mean you're stepping down from captain?"

Nico's eyebrows pull together, his dark gaze scanning mine. Although the freshman goalie hasn't said a word, I have a feeling he already knows where I'm going with this.

"No, I'm taking a break from varsity next year." I sigh, noting the look of horror creeping across Wes' face. Out of all my players, I knew he was going to take the news the hardest.

"I could give you a list of reasons why I am changing directions, but all you need to know is this is what I want to do. You boys will always be my team, that fact will never change, but it's about time I stepped back and worked on myself."

Nico nods, his eyes full of understanding, "You deserve to enjoy the rest of your university experience. Be able to take Stella dancing every weekend without worrying about upcoming tournaments."

I shoot him a smile, grateful for the support, "I am stupidly excited to have some free time. Speaking of which, with the new assistant coach next year, the next team captain shouldn't be as burdened as I was this year."

Nico gives Wes a nudge, but my favourite rookie is too busy being devasted to notice.

"It's not going to be the same without you."

"Of course not. Because the new captains are going to have their own approach to leadership and training."

Nico's eyes light up with surprise, "Captains? As in plural?"

I nod, "You and Wes will be co-captains starting next fall. That way, even if the assistant coach is a bust, the workload will be much more manageable split between two people." I chuckle, watching Wes' head whip back up in realization, "Plus, you both bring something special to the team. Between the two of you, I have faith there will be some balance between partying and actual practices."

Wes snaps upright with military position, "We won't let you down, Cap."

Nico nods, following his example with a salute, "It has truly been an honour."

I shake my head with a laugh, "Don't go sending me off to the gallows just yet. We've still got this year's tournament season to get through."

"Right, right." The newfound excitement buzzing through Wes makes it impossible for him to stand still.

Nico smirks and looks at me, "When do we find out who the new assistant coach will be?"

"My bet is the end-of-year banquet. That's when I will officially nominate you, so I would assume USport will make a similar announcement."

"Cool." Nico wiggles his eyebrows at his best friend, "I already have so many ideas for party themes."

I clear my throat and he throws me a wink, "Along with training drills, of course."

"Of course."

Wes widens his eyes in faux innocence, "In honour of Cap's departure, we should make a running program that only targets Hunter."

I laugh, "Now that would be a practice I would come back and watch."

Wes and Nico grin at each other, their playfulness and overall lack of serious intent solidifying my decision. It's easy to forget there are more important things than bringing home the championship banner, Mo and I have both been guilty of that, but leaving the future of Taber's lacrosse team with Wes and Nico has me confident that the next generation will keep a healthier balance.

That's the goal, anyway.

My train of thought derails when Wes steps forward and wraps me in a bear hug.

"I really am going to miss you, Cap."

I squeeze him back, chuckling when he tries and fails to lift me off the ground.

"I'm going to miss you too, Wes. You and Nico are going to make great captains."

He pulls away, green eyes shining, "You better not miss out on a single party next year."

Nico grins, "He won't. I know a certain platinum blonde who will drag his ass to every themed event she can find."

"That's true." I smile, thinking how my own future has never looked so promising, "I'm looking forward to seeing what you guys come up with."

"You already know I'm making a Pinterest board as soon as I get home."

I look at Nico in surprise, "You use Pinterest?"

"Hell yeah, where do you think all my great ideas come from?"

The three of us start heading towards the changeroom and Wes nods in confirmation, "Nico has a vision board for every opportunity. Even ones that aren't plausible."

Nico pouts, "Just because I sleep around doesn't mean I won't have a mini golden doodle ring bearer at my future wedding."

I blink, "That's specific."

"The heart wants what the heart wants." Nico shrugs, "Always thought I was a large dog kind of guy, but it turns out, those minis really grow on you."

Wes shakes his head, "Dude. You refused to go out with Luke yesterday because you said date conversation is boring."

"So? I'm not wrong."

"How do you expect to get married if you refuse to date anyone?"

Their friendly banter continues all the way to the showers, where I split off to have a moment of privacy. I pull my phone out of my pocket and smile at the name lighting up my notifications.

STELLA: How did it go???

STELLA: It's okay if you change your mind.

STELLA: I know those guys mean a lot to you.

If Stella isn't pacing her dorm right now then she has definitely found some sort of distraction. One that probably involves her poor roommate.

ME: It went better than expected. Wes and Nico are excited to be co-captains next year.

Stella had actually been the one to suggest the co-captain idea. When I had expressed concern about putting Lou and Wes' relationship in jeopardy if the captain position became too much to handle, she suggested breaking up the role between two people.

STELLA: Amazing. Any second thoughts??

At the start of this year, I thought I had to choose between Stella and her older brother. I thought I had to choose a side, decide where my loyalties lie and stand my ground. Now I realize that the decision was never going to be between Stella and Mo – It was never my loyalty that was the problem, it was my priorities.

In the end, it came down to choosing between Stella and lacrosse.

ME: Not a single one.

Stella

"Remind me again why you're straightening my hair?"

I smile, watching the steam drift from the iron in Lou's hair.

"Because you have a date tonight."

Lou frowns at me through the bathroom mirror, "But that isn't until this evening."

I carefully brush through the newly straightened strands, hunting for any stray pieces of wavy hair.

"Don't you and Wes have a class together this afternoon?"

"Yes, but what does that have to do with anything?"

I raise an eyebrow, "So you aren't going to have a quickie in the staff closet after human anatomy?"

Lou blushes, "We don't do that every time."

"Hm."

"We're just both really passionate about the topic."

I snort, "Passionate about Wes' anatomy, maybe."

"You got me."

We both crack up and I nearly burn Lou's hair in the process.

"Shit, sorry. You have to stop distracting me with these scandalous tales." Fumbling, I manage to get back on track and finish the rest of her head without incident.

"There. Let me just grab some hair spray to help hold it in place." I hurry to my room and return seconds later, surprised to see Lou nervously fiddling with her bracelet when I return.

The anxious look on her face is the same one she had when we first became friends, the social consciousness of someone uncomfortable in their own skin. It's pretty rare to see Lou revert back to her old tendencies, so whatever she's about to say is something that has been worrying her for a while.

"I was wondering... I don't really know how to say this." She hesitates, and I patiently wait for her to continue, "I know you and Cody are going strong now, and he has a house, so I totally understand if the answer is no, but..." Lou trails off, breaking eye contact to fiddle with her bracelet some more.

"What is it, Lou?"

"I was wondering if you would want to room with me next year?" She takes a deep breath, blurting out the next part so fast I almost miss it, "We can stay in residence or move off campus, it doesn't matter to me. I just don't feel ready to live with Wes yet and I don't know if I can handle another first day again."

I wait for her to take another gulping breath before patting her knee, "There is no one I would rather live with than you."

She smiles, halting the anxious fidgeting, "Really?"

"Really. Why don't we check out the housing applications this week and then decide to stay or leave campus?" I pull a face, "My only request is we find somewhere with bigger beds. The singles just aren't cutting it anymore."

Lou laughs, "They make sleepovers a little tough, for sure."

My mouth drops, "Sleepovers? I can barely fit in that bed by myself, how the hell do you have sleepovers in that thing?"

She shrugs, suddenly coy, "Wes and I make do."

I give my roommate a look of appreciation, "That might be my new favourite thing about you."

"That I can fit in a single bed with a lacrosse player?"

I shake my head, "That you're willing to be uncomfortable for the people you love."

We make eye contact in the mirror, and I hope she can see the appreciation for all the uncomfortable social situations she put herself through just so I could experience university the way my mother would have wanted me to.

"I mean, if you aren't uncomfortable, are you growing?"

I laugh at the quote, it's one I have heard and used too many times to count.

"Couldn't have said it better myself."

Chapter 29

2 months later...

Cody

"YOU'RE INSECURE, DON'T KNOW WHAT FOR."

The music blasts from my nightstand, jolting me straight out of a dead sleep.

What the hell?

"YOU'RE TURNING HEADS WHEN YOU WALK THROUGH THE DO-OR." I groan, reaching over and grabbing Stella's phone. One angry jab later and the One Direction song falls silent, leaving me staring groggily at the time on the screen. *4:30AM.*

"Stel, I think you forgot to-

I cut off abruptly, staring at the sleeping figure beside me. Her hair is strewn across my pillow, the comforter pulled up beneath her chin. Stella's chest rises and falls in time with her breathing, the peaceful look on her face making me want to snap a picture.

The scene is so serene that it takes me a minute to figure out what's missing. Then it hits me.

This is the first time Stella didn't wake up gasping for breath. It's the first time she has slept long enough to need the alarm I just turned off.

She'll be pissed if I don't wake her so we can hit the gym before the morning rush, but looking at her sleeping frame, there is no way I am ruining the leap of progress she just made.

Ever since that first therapy session, Stella has been attending weekly sessions over in Silverwood. It's tough to see internal progress, but she has seemed lighter these last few weeks. As if the past doesn't drag her down so much as keeps her grounded.

Quietly placing her phone back on the nightstand, I crawl back under the covers next to the girl who stole my heart that first day at the gym and hasn't given it back since.

Epilogue

♥

2 more months later...

Mo

It feels good to be back.

Looking around the poorly decorated banquet room, the scene looks identical to last year's lacrosse banquet and all the banquets before that. Taber dresses up the gymnasium to look semi-decent while athletes get respectably drunk in front of parents and guardians before throwing all respectability out the window the second their family members leave.

"Well, aren't you a sight for sore eyes." Mason's flaming red hair comes into my line of sight, and I hold back a grimace.

"Mason. Good to see your grades kept you around a while longer."

He grins like one of those annoying people who don't get offended, "Didn't want the shift from captains to be too dramatic after you left. Did you hear your protégé is giving up the title you so-kindly bestowed on him?"

What a dick.

"What Ellsworth does or doesn't do with his team has nothing to do with me." I nod towards the banner hanging next to the awards table, "Besides, it looks like he managed to get the job done even with your old ass holding back the team."

Mason laughs, "He sure did. Couldn't tell you how he pulled that one off, but he did."

I give him a cool nod before walking away. Some guys work their asses off, receive nothing in return, and take it like a champ. Mason was one of those people who got a chip on his shoulder whenever he was passed over for an award.

I have no patience for those people.

Girls smile in my direction as I make my way over to Stella and Cody's table, the coy looks and suggestive winks doing nothing to spark my interest. It's been a while since anyone intrigued me enough to take a second glance, but that doesn't stop me from pasting a smile on my face whenever someone looks my way.

I find my sister and Cody chatting amiably with another couple nearby. Cody's arm is wrapped protectively around Stella's waist, but I manage to spot the tattoo peeking out between the slit in her two-piece dress.

Falling beside Stella, I lean down to whisper in her ear.

"You're showing a lot of skin tonight."

She grins, shifting a long braid over her shoulder, "I'm working my way up to a bikini."

"Not for next year's banquet, I hope."

My sister laughs, looking more relaxed than I have seen her in a long time.

"Pretty sure father would disown me. Cody is planning a Banff getaway for us this summer, so the goal is to hit the hot springs wearing as little material as possible."

I chuckle, "In that case, keep the trip photos to yourself. There is only so much of you I want to see."

Stella slaps my arm, "Be nice."

Rambunctious laughter breaks out behind us, and we turn to see two rookies throwing chocolate covered fruit at each other. I raise my eyebrows and Stella sighs next to me.

"Don't be a douche, Mo."

"I didn't say anything."

She points at my expression, "Your face says it all."

Smoothing out my features, I give her a smile, "Better?"

"Much." Stella turns and rejoins the conversation around us while I observe the food fight going on in the corner. It's not so much a food fight as a try-and-catch-this-piece-in-your-mouth contest. I recognize the guy snatching fruit out of the air as Lou's boyfriend, Wes. The other one, the tall Latino throwing the food, is vaguely familiar but I don't immediately place him.

I sigh, turning away from the public display of immaturity and find Cody watching me closely.

"Yes?"

"You're looking good."

A smirk tugs my lips, "Ellsworth, you know I always look good."

Cody grins, "I meant you're looking lighter."

"Are you calling me fat?"

He rolls his eyes, "Between you and your sister, I don't know who likes to argue more. You seem less tense than the last time I saw you. Are you looking forward to the new position?"

"Temporary position." I correct him, "And yes, I am looking forward to taking a break from the boardroom."

Cody nods and looks away in thought. I catch his hand absently tracing Stella's scarred side and feel myself smile. There are some things in life that money can't buy, and the affection my friend showers over my sister is one of them.

"There's our new assistant coach!" Someone claps me on the back, and I turn to see the food thrower grinning at me.

"You ready to whip our team into shape?"

"Depends on whether the team is ready to be whipped into shape." I respond dryly, my eyes raking over the black silk shirt tucked neatly into pressed dressed pants. He's so close that I can smell the spice of his cologne, a fragrance that isn't unpleasant but needs to evacuate my personal space.

Immediately.

"Well, between the three of us, we should be able to get something done." He winks at me and all I can do is stare back.

"Why would we do anything together?" My tone is ice cold, my gaze equally hard as I silently tell this flamboyant rookie to *back the fuck off*.

"Did Cap not tell you?" He grins, as if sharing secrets is his favourite pastime, "Wes and I are going to be co-captains this fall. That means we'll be spending a lot of time together."

"And you are?" I reply coolly, refusing to let surprise show on my face. This will be the first year Taber has two captains instead of one, and based on the state of this half, it will also be the first year the Tigers don't bring home a banner.

"Nico Montez, at your service." Giving me an obvious once-over, Nico smirks, "And let me be the first to say, it would be my pleasure to service you."

I grit my teeth, staying silent. There is no use in engaging with a drunken flirt because it only encourages them. And Nico seems like the type who enjoys a reaction.

"Take it from a 10 to a 2, man." Wes materializes with Lou by his side. He shoots me an apologetic smile, "Nico gets a little carried away sometimes. Especially when he's had a lot to drink."

Nico shrugs, "Can't blame a guy for trying."

Ignoring him, I turn and give Wes' girlfriend a warm smile, "Looking lovely as ever, Lou. My sister is looking forward to living with you again next year."

Lou blushes from the base of her neck to the tips of her ears.

"I am looking forward to living with her too."

Wes takes her hand and squeezes it, the support flowing from his extraverted frame to her introverted one. At first glance, Wes and Lou seem like an odd match but the more I see them together, the more it makes sense.

Nico hoots behind me and goes running for someone across the room. My eyes follow his fumbling movements, the tight fit of his dress pants outlining the curve of his ass.

"Ten bucks says Lacey just arrived." Wes grins and gives Lou a peck on the cheek before holding out a hand for me to shake.

"Looking forward to having you assist in the fall."

I take his hand, "Likewise."

He and Lou disappear into the crowd, leaving me to my own devices. I snag a drink from a table nearby and find a seat away from the buzzing crowd.

Despite my best efforts, I find myself sneaking glances at Taber's new co-captain every few minutes, my restlessness growing.

Where have I seen him before?

Nico Montez flits around the room, pulling a young but gorgeous dark-haired girl through the crowd, introducing her to everyone with the same carefree abandon he used on me just moments earlier. His sexuality comes off in free, untamed waves that I hate to admire.

I'm about to take a sip of my drink when the DJ cues up a Spanish number. The familiar beat pulses through me and I freeze, clueing in to where I've seen Nico before.

"Oh my god! It's just like *Lifestyle*." Nico throws his head back and laughs, pulling the dark-haired girl towards the dance floor.

I down my drink just as a platinum braid comes into my line of sight.

"You ready to tear up the dance floor, big brother?" Stella holds out her hand and I take it, feeling the alcohol fill my veins with a much-needed buzz.

"Let's do it."

Together we head to the dance floor where I pretend this isn't the same song I danced to at Southern Alberta's rowdiest gay club.

Acknowledgements

The writing process for my debut novel was very much a learn-as-I-go-and-hope-for-the-best sort of situation but for Cody and Stella's story, I knew exactly where I wanted it to go. Each character is special, but these two gym gurus held a special place in my heart. I knew as soon as I introduced them in the first Taber Tigers that Cody and Stella deserved a chance to share their own story.

Plus, let's be honest: I have always been a sucker for a gym bro.

There are so many people I would like to thank for supporting me on this journey, I will do my best to include everyone but my apologies if I miss anyone!

A huge thank you goes to my younger brother, Logan. He was super salty he only got one line in the acknowledgements for the first novel, so I am making it up here. Stella and Mo's sibling relationship was one hundred percent inspired by the relationship I have with my own brother. Even though we are now adults, we still swing from good friends to mortal enemies but even at our worst moments there is unconditional love. Sibling relationships are a weird combination of intentional insults and tremendous support, and no one does that better than my brother.

Thank you, Dad, for the mindset and work ethic you taught me as a child. Jonathan O'Brien may have used some of your favourite quotes, but he lacked the support and love you always shared.

Thank you, Mom, for being the sole reason my debut novel released on-time with slightly less typos. Stella's mom was inspired by your love of dancing, and I hope those references put a smile on your face. You always go above and beyond for this family and for that, I thank you.

Thank you, Mara, for once again responding to all my updates even when you are in the middle of becoming a doctor. The fact you binged 60% of the first draft on the flight home attests to why you are my favourite.

Thank you, Christine, for not only reading my debut novel once but twice before jumping into the less edited version of this one. And let's not forget the D2L shoutout post you made for me this summer. You are my queen, my go-to dance partner, and a tremendous friend. Thank you again.

Thank you, Taylor P., for putting up with my continuous chatter about this book instead of letting you study. Thank you for taking the time to support me and for making my life in Lethbridge that much better.

Thank you, Taylor B., for ordering my book and sharing it with me during our teams meeting. You were the best part of last summer and I am so grateful to have gotten the chance to meet you. Team Marvel always.

Thank you, Elizabeth, for celebrating my debut with an endless transaction of daisies, love, and support. I can't wait for our next adventure.

Thank you, Angel, for reading my debut in 2 days and blushing through the sex scenes. Your enthusiasm meant more than words can say. I hope this one was worth the wait.

Thank you, Granny, for supporting my writing journey and for giving me the inspiration to live my life with no regrets. You are my role model.

Thank you, Grandma W., for not only reading my debut novel but buying a copy for all my cousins. Not sure they appreciated it, but I sure did.

Thank you, Gen and Micky, for the roommate memories we made these last few years. We definitely killed some brain cells watching those reality shows but it was worth it. Thank you both for supporting me on this journey.

Thank you, Joanne & Greg, for reading my debut and filling it with sticky notes. The Feddema clan is the best.

Thank you, Karena, for being my first ever Goodreads review. Sorry I keep sending more books your way.

A big thank you goes to my team last summer – Shelby, Erinn, Sophie, Taylor, and Cheryl – your enthusiasm for my book was amazing and I could not have asked for a better workplace experience. You are all rock stars.

Another big thank you goes to the book community on Instagram. So many of you took a chance on a new author and helped share my debut novel with the book world. Thank you for making my dream a reality.

To anyone who picked up this book and made it to the end. Thank you for choosing to spend your time reading Cody and Stella's story. I hope you found the break from reality you were looking for.

And lastly, celebrity shoutout to Sarina Bowen for showing me how addicting MM can be with *Him*. Thanks for being the first step in my research.

About the Author

Jade Everhart writes heart-warming romances with flawed characters and laugh-out-loud banter. When she's not using her own terrible meet-cutes as inspiration for her next novel, Jade spends her time listening to loud music and tearing up dance floors from the prairies of Southern Alberta to the glistening beaches of Miami.

Jade loves to hear from readers – connect with her on Instagram @authorjade_everhart.

Printed by Amazon Italia Logistica S.r.l.
Torrazza Piemonte (TO), Italy